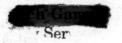

F/0232988

MISFIT LIL GETS EVEN

While Silver Vein's citizens watch 'Misfit Lil' shine in a gala shooting match, Yuma Nat Hawkins and his gang rob the bank and gun down the depleted opposition in cold blood. Patrick 'Preacher' Kilkieran witnesses the robbery, but keeps his distance — and is soon striking a mysterious deal with a renegade Indian before fleeing town. But it's Kilkieran's brutal assault on Lil's friend Estelle that compels her to vow retribution and track him down . . .

CHAP O'KEEFE

MISFIT LIL GETS EVEN

Complete and Unabridged

LINFORD
Leicester

First published in Great Britain in 2006 by
Robert Hale Limited
London

First Linford Edition
published 2008
by arrangement with
Robert Hale Limited
London

British Library CIP Data

O'Keefe, Chap
    Misfit Lil gets even.—Large print ed.—
Linford western library
    1. Western stories
    2. Large type books
    I. Title
    823.9'14 [F]

    ISBN 978–1–84782–053–2

Published by
F. A. Thorpe (Publishing)
Anstey, Leicestershire

Set by Words & Graphics Ltd.
Anstey, Leicestershire
Printed and bound in Great Britain by
T. J. International Ltd., Padstow, Cornwall

This book is printed on acid-free paper

1

DAY MADE FOR ROBBERY

The double crack was brittle and explosive. Bright shards of green glass cascaded out of a grey-blue sky. They caught and accentuated the light of a sun made watery by thin cloud that hinted at the coming of an early, cold winter. Nearby willows were turning gold; more distantly, maples' flame gave foothills the redness suggestive of a banked-up hell.

But for now the crowd was forgetful of nature's coming trials. Here was the fun of a fair, flags flapping in a stiffening breeze, tents and banners of many colours. And the thrill and excitement of a shooting match. The happy folk roared approval as the ninety-first thrown bottle smashed.

'Every one a bull's-eye!'

'Pity the poor idiots who didn't bet on Misfit Lil!' Wherever they'd put their money, the crowd's delight had an extra edge because the final round after an elimination contest was being fought out between a male and a female shooter: Corporal Harry Hollings, best marksman of Fort Dennis, and Miss Lilian Goodnight, harum-scarum daughter of rancher Ben Goodnight, known popularly as Misfit Lil.

Lieutenant Michael Covington looked on and inwardly fretted. Lil hadn't missed a single bottle, and seven of her ten had now been thrown. Since Hollings had missed his fourth, she had only to hit each of her last three to be declared winner.

Hollings caught Covington's stern eye and tried to suppress his scowl. To rub salt in the wound, the contest rules had left the firearm to the entrant's choice or the dictate of his finances. Hollings was equipped with a fine new, army-purchased rifle. It had been supplied not by the United States Armoury in Springfield, Massachusetts, home of the single-shot Trap Door Springfield, but by the Winchester Repeating Arms Company, and it was said to be the latest improvement on its famous Model '73.

Meanwhile, the brat Lilian Goodnight was relying on a pair of old Colt revolvers with much-worn wooden handles. Yet victory and the army's honour were still slipping from Hollings' grasp as the empty centre-fire shells were spat from the Winchester's breech to spot the stomped ochre ground around his shiny black cavalry boots like metallic hail.

The day of the fall gala was a red-letter day in the Silver Vein social calendar. Leastways, Colonel Brook Lexborough, the grizzled commanding officer at Fort Dennis, had told Lieutenant Covington he saw it that way.

Covington's private view was that the frontier ranching and mining town had nothing as grand as a social calendar. Indeed, it was a wonderment to him that the unruly town had managed to organize a gala. It had failed utterly to replace satisfactorily its former sheriff — a man implicated in murder and the sale of guns and whiskey to a bunch of renegade Apaches — and the military's operations had since largely devolved to compensating for the inadequacies of civilian law enforcement as shakily practised by the new, weakling incumbent of the sheriff's office.

On this day, the lieutenant would have preferred to be leading a detail to continue the fight against Angry-he-shakes-fist, Apache sub-chief and leader of the rebels who'd broken out of the reservation. Instead, he was watching a shoot — a game.

In his wisdom Colonel Lexborough had sent Covington to fly the army's flag at the tinpot gala. Young and clean-cut, he was a dashing figure in his smart uniform; though it wasn't his intention, he had a useful propensity for making the ladies ooh and aah.

Just about everybody who was

anybody in or around Silver Vein had gathered for the event on the bare sage flat across the willow-choked creek from town, leaving only the old, the infirm, the most oppressed workers and the confirmed kill-joys in their customary posts, their habitual haunts.

Misfit Lil barked again to her assistant in her best unladylike manner. '*Throw . . .*'

Covington winced in distaste.

★   ★   ★

While the bottles soared to their destruction and the crowd's applause, the township of Silver Vein slumbered.

Typically, old Moses Goldberg sat dozing on a stool behind the counter in his emporium, alone in the pungent silence of leather goods and coffee beans, coal oil and other mingled, heady odours. Arthritis in his legs would have made closing his store and attending the gala a source of pain rather than pleasure.

Next door, P.J. Richardson, morose, overweight proprietor of Richardson's Hardware, was taking advantage of the lull in business to rearrange his back storeroom and was cursing a spilled keg of nails.

Across the main drag, in the Ranchers' and Miners' Bank, three bored employees, denied the chance to attend the festivities, showed a little more life. They'd dared to produce a deck of cards for their entertainment.

They were Seth Whitfield, teller, George Massey, bookkeeper, and Eddie Chaney, his assistant.

Further along the street, on the side of the emporium and hardware store, Martha Coutts — 'Ma' Coutts — who owned and managed the Traveller's Hotel, best hostelry Silver Vein could boast, was laying tables in her restaurant in between preparing supper food in her kitchen. She could scarcely give the afternoon off to herself as well as 'her girls'.

On a balcony of the hotel, overlooking the street, a guest, Patrick Kilkieran, often called the Preacher in recognition that he'd once been ordained a priest, lazed deceptively in a rocker while he mentally reviewed the ambitious plans and options that had brought him into this country.

Around three in the afternoon, seven men rode quietly into Silver Vein in two separate bunches after waiting unseen in woods east of the town. Each man wore a long, linen duster which hid a well-stocked cartridge belt and a pair of heavy revolvers in well-oiled holsters.

The first bunch, of three, came in openly and dismounted outside the bank. The clop of hoofs, creak of leather and clink of saddle bits drew the attention of Moses Goldberg who limped to the door of his emporium and watched the trio throw their horses' reins over the hitch rail, then enter the bank building. Old Moses frowned, at a loss to place the arrivals — they were no customers he recognized — and stayed where he was, one gnarled hand gripping the door jamb to take his weight.

The other four of the seven emerged from an alley. One swung down from his horse in the middle of the street and made a show of adjusting his saddle's stirrup assembly. Another dismounted but left his horse unhitched and began pacing nervously up and down outside the bank. The remaining pair stayed mounted and watchful.

It wasn't only Moses who watched the arrivals and found the situation suspicious.

Up on the hotel balcony, Kilkieran ceased his gentle rocking. His eyes widened. Agog, he waited, silent and unmoving.

If I don't miss my guess, he thought, *one of those fellers carries himself just like Yuma Nat Hawkins.*

This could be mighty interesting. Yuma Nat was the hard and cruel boss of the desolate outlaw country south of Silver Vein and Kilkieran understood he was widely respected and feared. The territory was such that many of the local ranchers tolerated outlawry. Also, Yuma Nat was reckoned too big to waste time on rustling the ranchers' piddling bunches of cattle and horses. These days, he was set up to give sanctuary at his hideout to fugitives passing through — 'long as they paid, of course — and he robbed trains. And banks . . .

But Kilkieran knew him of old. Kilkieran had been born of Irish Catholic parents at an old mission in San Francisco. He'd rebelled in his youth, taken up with a Barbary Coast gang and wandered the West. During this spell of his life, before his ordination, Kilkieran had passingly associated with Yuma Nat and his gang of the time.

If he could glimpse the face of the suspected man he'd seen go into the bank, Kilkieran would know for sure. For an old scar puckered one cheek and twisted Yuma Nat's mouth in a frozen grin-cum-grimace that made him instantly identifiable, though his moods and thoughts tricky to judge.

Down at street level, Moses Goldberg gathered what he had of public spirit, coupled it with the knowledge his business had a healthy sum deposited in the bank, and decided to ask questions. Leaving the sanctuary of his store, he lurched across to the Ranchers' and Miners' Bank.

The nervous man stopped pacing, let his duster fall open and drew a revolver.

'Stand still, mister! You ain't goin' in there. Stand still!'

The shocked storekeeper acted automatically and maybe foolishly. Face white as chalk, he turned on an unsteady heel and tried to run, hollering, 'Help! They're robbing the bank. Get your guns, folks!'

Simultaneously, a shot rang out from inside the building. This decided the jittery man who'd drawn on Goldberg; the jig was up and the gang could do without his cries spreading explanation and raising other opposition. He raised his pistol and fired.

Goldberg had taken less than a half-dozen jerky strides. The heavy slug punched into his back, severing his spine, ripping through his body to emerge in a pulpy gout of flesh and blood from his chest. He was flung — headlong, face-first and dead — into the dust and his arthritic legs kicked their last in grotesque reflex.

P.J. Richardson came through from his back room, assessed the scene on the street and reached under his counter where he had stashed a double-barrelled shotgun and a supply of buckshot shells.

Ma Coutts went to her restaurant window, flung up her hands and shrieked.

Above, Patrick Kilkieran licked his dry lips. His hands rasped as he rubbed them together. He made no move to arm himself or leave his hotel balcony.

★　★　★

Jackson Farraday watched Misfit Lil acknowledge the cheers of the crowd and go over to shake the gauntleted hand of the crestfallen Corporal Hollings.

Farraday was a weather-burnished scout and guide — a civilian who worked on occasion with the army. He commiserated with Lieutenant Michael Covington.

Shaking his head of long, sun-bleached hair wonderingly, he said, 'Your soldier-boy never had a prayer, Lieutenant. Everyone knows Miss Goodnight can hit a dime at a hundred feet. They don't call her the Princess of Pistoleers without good reason.'

'Hmph! Princess is no word I'd use to describe her, Mr Farraday. Like always, she's turned out today dressed worse than a saddle-tramp. It's a calculated insult. Immodest!'

Thoughtfully, Jackson scratched his jaw, cleanshaven except for a neat chin-beard. He took stock of Misfit Lil's dress, mentally noting it was familiar enough to both himself and Covington.

12

Lil favoured men's clothing. She wore a well-fitting, fringed buckskin shirt and a pair of Levi's stout work pants, reinforced with more buckskin sewn around the crotch and inside legs. Her heavy six-guns nestled in the holsters of a wide belt slung low on her hips. She had glossy black hair, and one touch of colour, though not especially feminine, was a red bandanna. She was tall for a girl, reaching a height above Jackson's own shoulders.

'Now have a heart, Lieutenant,' he said. 'It ain't often these days that the gal gets to wear those duds, and you know how high she sets 'em above the blouses and skirts she has to wear at the Traveller's Hotel.'

Jackson was twice Lil's age — he reckoned she'd seen eighteen-some summers — and though his own occasional censure wasn't as serious as that professed by Mike Covington, he, too, regarded her with good cause as a pest. Nevertheless, he felt sorry for the girl.

Lil had grown up to become a crack shot good as any of her father's punchers, an expert rider, roper of calves and driver of cows. But her pa, against the will of his spirited, outdoors daughter, had sent her to Boston for refinement and education as dispensed by a high-toned boarding-school.

What Lil did next, involving a willing gardener's-boy, got her expelled. Word of her indelicate exploits came back with her to the Silver Vein country. Folk stopped calling the respected Mr Goodnight's daughter 'Miss Lilian'. It became 'Misfit Lilian': then simply 'Misfit Lil'. The girl was too feisty to repent of or change her ways, and her despairing father disowned her.

Jackson knew Lil would rather ride the wilderness trails, living largely off the land and emulating the scouting life of himself, whom she hero-worshipped. Yet thorough familiarity with this land she loved had told her winter in it could be severe. The season's approach had forced her to start working as a waitress at the hotel. She apparently counted herself lucky to have secured the live-in position for the while, since it freed her from having to crawl back to her pa at the Flying G ranch and admit the error of her ways.

Thus Jackson appreciated she would have doubly enjoyed the freedom of the gala today to express her true self and show off her real skills.

All this he understood, but Covington's disappointment with the outcome caused him to persist.

'Well, it's a generous thing Ma Coutts has taken young Goodnight in. I hope she's taken her in hand, too.'

'Could be. I do hear tell the girls she takes on live under a strict regime. She sees they're in their rooms by ten and go to prayer meetings Wednesday nights.'

Their exchange was picked up by Misfit Lil's sharp ears.

'Not so much of the young, Mike. You ain't so much older your own self, and you missed out on four years of real living while you were at West Point.'

Covington stiffened with anger, especially when she addressed him by the diminutive of his given name — he considered this bad manners — but Lil was turning now to Jackson.

'And no, I don't like wearing a blouse and skirt, curfews or prayer meetings. But it gets balanced by Ma letting us go to a Saturday night dance.'

Jackson found himself nodding affirmatively. The Traveller's Hotel was famed near and moderately far for its fine accommodations, its food and its comely waitresses, known as 'Ma's girls'.

The dance date undoubtedly appealed to the young, single women Martha Coutts aimed to employ as her girls. Her basic requirements were natural prettiness and willingness to stay unmarried and work for six months. But the spinster hotelier was no tyrant; Jackson suspected she had past sadness in her life and her own secrets. In line with this, she turned a blind eye to

16

consenting liaisons between her girls and patrons, as long as no girl fell pregnant and matters were kept decorous and discreet; as long as no harm was done to her business.

Lil went on, 'Of course, if some worthy person would offer me a decent alternative before next year . . . ' Expressive grey eyes fixed Jackson's pale blue-grey with a steady beseeching gaze.

Jackson felt uncomfortable. He found Lil physically attractive, but considered any relationship deeper than friendship would be inappropriate and a taking of advantage. Being an idol was a bother to him. Not for the first time, he thought why couldn't Lil and Michael Covington settle their differences? They were of an age to make a good, complementary match.

He forced a laugh. 'Enough funning, Miss Lilian. You'll embarrass the lieutenant here.'

Covington said, 'My observation, Miss Goodnight, tells me a proper gentleman will only approach a lady after she has acquired some social graces.'

Hollings was shifting from foot to foot in discomfiture at the clash threatening between his superior and his better in marksmanship.

Lil just gasped. 'My, ain't you the stuffed shirt? No, a uniform draped on a manual of etiquette and regulations. Why, if the corporal here wants to go to the latrines, I bet you'll insist on written orders in triplicate and the colonel's signature!'

The call for retaliation to her sassing got the better of Covington's ruffled composure.

'A local tall tale has it you were bitten lately by a rattler, missy. I'm minded to believe the windy's payoff — the snake died, you lived.'

'Oh, that's *poisonous*, Mike Covington!' Lil quickly retorted.

How the back-chat would have continued, Jackson was never to know. Sudden gunfire was heard from the direction of town, and the exchange and the crowd's background hubbub abruptly broke off.

The momentary silence was succeeded by shouts of alarm and urgent consultation.

'What the hell's that? Who's left in town to be firin' guns?'

'Never mind who! It ain't anythin' that c'n be right.'

Jackson said to Covington, 'Order every available man to town double-quick!'

Lil whooped. 'Hurry, boys, hurry!'

The gala was over. A rush to horses was made by all who'd brought them.

2

WATCHER IN THE SHADOWS

When Yuma Nat Hawkins and two of the hardest of his hardcases strode into the Ranchers' and Miners' Bank, guns drawn, they received an educational experience of sorts, never having encountered book-keepers or tellers engaged in poker for the smallest of stakes in the middle of an empty banking chamber.

But Yuma Nat wasn't as surprised as Messrs Whitfield, Massey and Chaney. They dropped their hands and goggled. 'Uh?' and 'Mmm?' was as much as they could muster.

'Don't nobody holler; don't nobody make a false move! We're takin' the pot, gents,' Yuma Nat said.

One of his sidekicks reached for the small stack of coin and bills on the table and teller Whitfield pushed it toward him with a shaky but practised hand.

'Naw, not that one,' Yuma Nat said coldly. 'You think I got forty guns waitin' outside for that penny-ante stuff?'

'N-no,' Whitfield stammered, while the sidekick in error made a quick recovery and waved his gun menacingly.

'Are you the head cashier?' Yuma Nat asked.

'No!' Whitfield said, this time more firmly.

Yuma Nat put the question to bookkeeper Massey. 'Are you?'

The pasty-faced man shook his head from side to side and moaned, 'I don't wanna die.'

The outlaw who'd accepted their small change sniggered. 'Ev'ry mother's son's gotta die sometime.'

Yuma Nat put his question the third time. 'Are you?'

Massey's assistant, Chaney, licked his lips. 'Swear I ain't, mister.'

Turning again to Whitfield, the most senior in years, Yuma Nat roared, 'You are the cashier! We're robbin' this goddamn bank — open the safe quick or I'll blast your head off.'

The door to the unfrequented bank's vault had been left open by the disgruntled, negligent trio obliged to man it by an unsympathetic manager who'd gone to the gala. Yuma Nat's second sidekick had moved over to the vault and stepped within to look around.

Affecting to follow Yuma Nat's instructions, Whitfield moved swiftly to the heavy door and tried to close it on the outlaw.

'Hey! I said no tricks, lunkhead!' Yuma Nat cuffed Whitfield with his gun barrel; dragged him back with the help of his first pard. Blood trickled down the side of Whitfield's face from a split over his ear.

Yuma Nat thrust the muzzle of his gun into his face. 'We ain't foolin'. Open the safe now, or you're a dead man!'

Whitfield tried to keep his head at the same time as he considered the prospect of losing it.

'The safe's fitted with a time lock. I can't open it any time soon.'

Yuma Nat had heard robbery victims' lies before — many times. He figured this was one. He'd wanted to carry out this gala-day raid quietly, without firing a shot, but the strategy plainly wasn't going to work. So he switched to the back-up plan. Act violently and swiftly and get the hell out while the numbers were on his gang's side.

Cursing, he put his gun alongside Whitfield's battered head and pulled the trigger. Dazed, Whitfield slumped to the floor, stunned by the blast.

This was the shot heard outside by the jittery outlaw who proceeded to gun down the hollering Moses Goldberg. But it worked insofar as it drained the last of the fight from Whitfield. Whimpering, he worked the combination dial and the safe door swung open.

Massey and Chaney were ordered to kneel behind the main counter while the robbers emptied the safe into gunny sacks. Yuma Nat was pondering the meaning of the second shot, in the street, and getting anxious to ride out — fast, before the town was peopled by more than the halt and the lame.

His plans could swiftly be reduced to a farrago if the gala crowd came storming back into Silver Vein as he and his boys were quitting the town.

His mind a mess of distraction, Yuma Nat didn't notice that the kneeling Chaney, remembering a loaded pistol he kept in a drawer for emergencies that never happened, had edged his way to it. In agitation, Chaney fumbled the gun out, cocked it, jumped to his feet and made a dash for the manager's deserted office at the bank's rear.

One of the bandits gave belated chase. He hurtled through the office door. Chaney had jumped on to a desk. He'd opened a window and was fiddling to unlock the grille that covered the

24

escape route. Both men fired.

Chaney, hit in the chest, smashed through the window frame and glass. The bars beyond swung wide, either already unlatched or ripped loose by the impact. He toppled from sight in the explosion of debris.

Chaney's bullet entered the robber at the collar-bone. It glanced off, tore through muscle and exited from his right shoulder. He returned to the banking chamber, clutching a bloody wound.

Yuma Nat saw red. He got ruthless.

'The game's up, fellers. We've got more money'n we c'n carry. Better light a shuck!'

He pumped shots at the other bank workers, hitting Whitfield in the thigh and Massey in the leg. 'I can't trust yuh'll allow this withdrawal without interferin'.'

The three bank raiders raced out, anxious to leap astride their waiting horses. Before they reached the hitch-rail, they stopped in their tracks, confronted by the hardware store's proprietor, P.J. Richardson, approaching ponderously. He raised his formidable double-barrelled shotgun, tucking the stock against his shoulder.

Loaded with money bags, Yuma Nat cursed, 'For Christ's sake, put him down!'

One of the two outlaws who'd stayed patrolling the street on horseback raised a pistol and fired. Its crack was drowned out by a tremendous roar as Richardson pulled the front trigger of the big shotgun. He was struck by the bullet from behind at the same time. The scatter-gun's muzzle swung wildly and the scythe of big buckshot mostly sliced the flank and rump of one of the standing horses and peppered the bank's frontage.

Richardson and the horse went down as the echoes racketed through the street. The hardware man was dead; the horse threshed its limbs and squealed horribly. No one bothered to put it out of its agony.

'Hot damn! Ain't this a hell of a note?' Yuma Nat said indignantly.

'Whadda we do, Nat?' one of his sidekicks asked.

'Yuh'll have to ride double,' Yuma Nat told them. 'This is serious trouble, but needs be we'll shoot our way out yet. Thar's only ol' fools an' deadbeats in town. Most likely, they'll stay outa sight.'

Four men climbed into saddles, the outlaw with the shoulder wound mounted up behind, and the whole bunch heeled their six surviving horses into motion and clattered down the main drag.

* * *

High on the front balcony of the Traveller's Hotel, Patrick Kilkieran drew back where he was less obvious from the street yet retained a comprehensive view. Kilkieran reckoned the secret to living a long and profitable life in frontier towns was to pick carefully the times when you interfered in the lives of others.

He couldn't care less that he'd witnessed the cold-blooded killing of two citizens, lying in pools of blood on the street outside the bank. Likely others had died, too, inside the building.

What was happening in half-empty Silver Vein was none of Kilkieran's business, but he was alert to the possibility that he might make it such in later and more favourable circumstances.

The fleeing band swept past below him. The cloud of dust that rose from the thundering hoofs of their horses didn't obscure the face of their leader. Yuma Nat Hawkins for a plumb certainty! No two men could have the same hideous face, half-frozen by the ravages of an old knife-fight wound.

So that was it, thought Kilkieran: Yuma Nat had pulled off another bank robbery, right under his nose but nary another fit and capable soul's . . .

But no, what was this?

A block down at the intersection of a

cross-street, Yuma Nat and his boys were pulling up, tugging their horses' tossing heads up and round, dancing them sideways and turning about.

Kilkieran heard snorting through distended nostrils, a jingle of bit-pieces — and a disgusted cry.

'South ain't no use, boys — the townies are comin' back with the goddamn bluebellies!'

Several horsemen were already entering the main stem, including a girl Kilkieran recognized; one of Ma Coutts's cavvy of tempting fillies — the spirited one they called Misfit Lil and said knew this country like the back of her hand, but who seemed kinda out of place in a hotel and who'd rejected his advances forcefully.

On horseback, urging the cayuse forward with a flip of rein ends and dressed in buckskin, the insolent girl did look to be in her natural element. Regrettably, she was different from all other girls he'd known in other ways, too.

The bandits, on a return run, drew level with the hotel. Ma Coutts ran out on to the street. She was wringing her hands and pleading inarticulately. When she almost threw herself in front Yuma Nat's horse, Kilkieran thought the outlaw boss would surely shoot her down. What did the stupid old cow think she could do?

Yuma Nat could as well have ridden her down under the trampling hoofs, but he swerved his horse around her.

'Git outa the road, Ma!' he yelled, and the astounding, dangerous moment passed. The cavalcade stormed on unopposed, stirrup to stirrup, leaving Silver Vein by the opposite route north.

The army detail was all in dress uniform. Plainly to Kilkieran, it had been showing the colours at the gala to impress the locals. When it reached the hotel, its leader reined in. 'Whoa!' he ordered, raising a hand. 'Company, halt!'

Black hair swirling, Misfit Lil turned on him. 'Why are we stopping, Mike?

We gotta round up those evil bastards! The bank's been robbed. Look — dead men are lying on the street!'

'It's not the army's job, Miss Goodnight,' the lieutenant informed her, his tone curt. 'Our duty is to maintain the peace and bring about national unity. Chasing criminals is primarily the role of the civilian authorities. Sheriff Hamish Howard must raise a posse.'

'Good God! You know how long the incompetent weakling will take to get around to that. The gang'll be vanished into the mountains and the winter. C'mon, fellers, let's ride on!'

The lieutenant's face reddened. 'Everybody, hold fast!' He shook his finger at the girl. 'You'll not interfere, missy!'

No one moved.

'Oh, get a cinch on your temper, Mike!' the girl said with a fiery flicker of her own. 'I guess they're gonna get away now anyhow. To stick to your straight soldiering and the formalities, you've squandered our chance.'

Kilkieran watched the party break up and go its separate ways.

Yuma Nat's gang was going to get off scot-free, it looked like. Which was just dandy in his book.

* * *

Not much later, Misfit Lil was back in blouse and skirt as one of 'Ma's girls'. She might as well be wearing a strait jacket was her rueful opinion. Her head still reeled madly from the excitement of the wild ride back to town and the dissatisfaction of its abrupt denouement. Her victory in the shooting match was all but forgotten; its pleasure quite overwhelmed by annoyance with Mike Covington.

Jackson Farraday, bless him, had tried to console her.

'You were right, of course, but the lieutenant has to consider his position. He walks a fine line here, and you know how wedded he is to doing the right thing. Fort Dennis was established in response to the Indian troubles. Other outlawry is a side issue.'

Lil was aware that, despite his mild reaction to the aborted chase and his attempt at conciliation, Jackson shared her frustration over the set ways of the military. He was a man of vastly more experience than Mike Covington — a frontier scout and guide, the real article. The army hired him, civilian though he was, for his knowledge and ability, usually by the month and for specific expeditions.

He'd hunted buffalo and supplied meat for railroad construction workers; he'd carried dispatches through hostile Indian country; he was a remarkable man of unexpectedly wide education, said to be fluent in seven languages and several Indian dialects. He also understood the Indians' situation better than most of his peers.

Lil had witnessed, too, that just like herself Jackson didn't always see eye to eye with the military — especially inexperienced young lieutenants.

'Hmm,' she had said with a measure of scorn. 'Can we be sure Mike Covington knows what to do about the Indians? He hasn't brought in Angry-fist yet, has he?'

The vainglorious Apache and his marauding party of rebellious young bucks were still hiding out in the bleak canyonlands and attracting new defectors from the reservation. This, despite the loss of Angry-fist's left hand in a tomahawk duel with Jackson.

Jackson had shaken his head wisely.

'We're in no position to judge what's inaction and what's not. A soldier's job is to carry out orders, not question them. I hear the latest orders from the Department of State are not to fight the Indians unless attacked. The army is here to protect them, not to provoke matters and fan a spark of individual rebellion into the flames of a new war.'

Misfit Lil was jerked out of her contemplations by a peremptory summons from a corner table of the restaurant.

'Over here, girlie!' Patrick Kilkieran called. 'You can have my order right now.' He produced one of his spurious laughs. 'Mebbe I'll have another for you . . . like, sit on my knee and tell me about the gala and the spat with the pompous bluecoat you rode back with in such a rush!'

Now here was an aggravation of an altogether different sort. Misfit Lil reviewed it glumly . . .

3

UNWELCOME ATTENTIONS

Patrick Kilkieran had arrived in Silver Vein on a Concord drawn by a team of fast-running blacks. He'd boarded the stagecoach at Green River, having come west out of Colorado by the Denver & Rio Grande Western Railway.

He stepped on pointed, calf-length boots into Ma Coutts's Traveller's Hotel and swaggered up to the front-lobby desk like he owned the place and everyone in it. Above the boots, he was wearing a dark broadcloth suit, a flashy waistcoat, a string tie — all mussed some by travel.

He had a pair of cat-yellow, heavy-lidded eyes.

Misfit Lil took a dislike to him from the start. It wasn't that he was unhandsome as older men — which to her was men over thirty — went. Most any woman under sixty could be excused for looking at Kilkieran twice. He was sleek and proud in an animal fashion. But he was also too alert, too hard.

'Who does he think he is?' she muttered to Ma Coutts.

'Hush your mouth, gal!' the shrewd hotelier hissed. 'That's Preacher Kilkieran.'

And who the hell was Preacher Kilkieran?

'He don't look like a preacher,' she told the matriarch once the guest was upstairs removing the grime of his long ride on public conveyances.

Ma Coutts was a grey-haired woman of uncertain years with broad hips and shoulders, a solicitous way and some seeming sorrow . . . but stern with it.

'Mebbe so. He ain't a priest any more,' she said.

'Well, that don't surprise me,' Lil said. 'The way he looked me up and down would've been enough to get him defrocked.'

Ma huffed. 'Young gals shouldn't be hasty in their judgements,' she lectured. 'Mr Kilkieran is said to have done good works. He broke away from popery to follow wider religious and scientific interests. He studied at the Transylvania Medical School in Lexington, Kentucky. Then, being blessed as a healer, he set up one of them colonies in Colorado, Pure Waters Colony.'

'Like General Palmer's Fountain Colony?'

'I reckon that's so. Rich sick folks go there for the dry and healthful climate and to drink and bathe in the springs' waters. To take the cure. Specially when they got weak lungs and breathing troubles.'

Lil shrugged. She was used to being stared at by all sorts. It came with her reputation and the mannish clothes she wore against convention when she was her own person. Though she didn't think of herself as pretty, maybe her natural fitness and tallness also made part of the package that drew folks' attention. She often felt remote from town life, as untamed as the wild country around it in which she felt at home.

On his second day in Silver Vein, Lil went to collect the empty supper dishes from Kilkieran's table in the restaurant, and he asked her brazenly, 'Would you care to step up with me to my room?'

He'd been drinking copiously with his meal but wasn't drunk, just hot and flushed.

Lil knew that Ma Coutts' rules neither forbade nor called for fraternizing with guests. The choice was hers. She didn't want to fan the fire of passion; she knew what happened to moths that flew too close to flames. But she was curious about Preacher Kilkieran. What was a visionary developer doing in this unlikely territory?

Responding to his overtures, at least in appearance, might pay her back in information. Getting to the bottom of the mystery of his presence in Silver

Vein before anyone else would be a satisfying coup.

She also thought she was competent to handle any alcoholic fumblings of an intimate nature. She'd let him make his play, then put him down in a crushing way that would put paid to his unwelcome attentions once and for all. Get it right out of his overheated system.

Kilkieran's room was the best in the house. It had a double bed with a feather mattress, armchairs, a mahogany dresser and wardrobe, the biggest washstand with the best porcelain water pitcher and bowl and a pile of fluffy towels.

'Come right on in, honey,' Kilkieran said. 'I want to have a . . . talk.'

Lil cringed at the 'honey' — she was that to no one ever — but she said brightly, 'Oh, yes, sir. A talk would be lovely. I want you to tell me all about yourself.'

He laughed in a self-congratulatory way at her cooperative manner. 'Sure, missy. You can call me Patrick and I'll call you Lil. I can see we're going to be very friendly.'

He shut the door after them firmly.

Lil was nothing if not forthright. 'What are you doing in this country, Patrick?'

He lit a lamp with an amber-tinted glass chimney and turned the wick low.

'Sure you are an inquisitive girl, Lil,' he said. 'But draw those window curtains — like the good girl ev'ryone seems to reckon you ain't! — and, since I want you to help, I'll tell.'

She drew the curtains quickly, without arguing anything, not wanting to turn her back to him for too long, and he went on.

'You've also no small name in these parts for knowing the lie of the land — as good, I do hear say, as that scout feller the army uses — Jackson Farraday. I can use such talents, Lil, and I'd prefer them to be in a delectable shape like your own rather than Mr Farraday's.'

Lil glowed with pride at the first compliment; to be as good a frontier guide as her hero was all she aspired to. The second piece of flattery rang warning bells.

'What is it you want done, Patrick?'

'I'm about to mount a personal exploration of the mountains hereabout for a site suitable for developing into a new and grander resort than Pure Waters Colony. Your thorough familiarity with the terrain could aid the location of springs with a whiff of sulphur, a hint of minerals.'

Lil frowned. 'I don't know there are such places, though the water at some of the secret holes the Indians use can taste awful strange.'

'That doesn't deter me.' Kilkieran drew closer to Lil. He studied what he could see of her legs, which wasn't much below the calf-length hem of her skirt, then let his eyes travel up her body to meet her eyes. 'In fact, I see promise . . . '

'Ho, you do, do you? Well, what

about them Indians? You must've heard Angry-fist and his murdering rebels are still hiding out in the canyon-lands. He lost a hand in combat with Mr Farraday, but that ain't slowed him down too much. He's fiercer than ever. He'd as soon take your scalp as anybody's, 'cept Jackson's, of course, which he really covets.'

'That doesn't scare me. As a religious man at core, and a healer, I can appreciate many of the Indians' beliefs and customs. They're genuine, sincere. They've a better working relationship with the Great Spirit — that is, with Yosen, or whatever name they give him. Their religion's without the hypocrisy which bedevils white men.'

Kilkieran was continuing to edge in on her as he spoke. Lil backed off till she was trapped up against the big bed. But she could hold her own in any debate he cared to instigate. She found herself starting to gabble, if only to distract him from the purpose she figured he had in mind.

'I don't have much time for churches myself, if that's what you mean,' she agreed. 'I figure the redskins have it right. The Creator's masterpiece is the outside, in the high mountains and on the vast prairie, and those are the holy places where you should give praise for His works, watched maybe by the deer and the antelope, the bear . . . the odd buffalo herd. Not some musty church or mission building. But weren't you a priest once?'

' "Woe unto them that call evil good, and good evil; that put darkness for light . . . that put bitter for sweet",' he quoted obliquely. 'That was just a passing enthusiasm.'

Lil wondered how many of those he'd had. She reckoned he was a hypocrite himself, and a quack. Moreover, she never trusted people who quoted or misquoted Scripture by way of mocking her. The headmistress at a certain seminary for young ladies in Boston had had a habit of doing that and it brought back memories of being thrown out in disgrace, though no one had gotten hurt by her behaviour.

'Well, that's as maybe,' she said. 'Aside from Injuns, there's winter coming on. Utah in winter ain't friendly to tenderfoot travellers.'

He regarded her from slightly hooded eyes. 'I'm no tenderfoot, Lil. In my past, I've done a fair share of riding lonely trails. You could say I'm an experienced man on every count, and I've the money to make it worth your while . . . '

'I see.'

He was too close to her; she was too near to him. She was aware of the liquor fumes on his breath, which was quickened and shallow.

'Did you never hear what happened to the men who worked for the government mail contractor George Chorpenning?' she pressed on. 'It was before the War Between the States but my father told me, and the winter weather ain't no diff'rent yet. They had their horses and mules frozen to death in the Goose Creek Mountains, had to strap their mail pouches on their backs, trudged on foot two hundred mile to Salt Lake City. They ate mule meat till it gave out, six days off the end of a fifty-three-day trek. Setting out now would be plumb foolish — Patrick . . . '

She faltered to a halt. He was taking no notice of a word she was saying. He took her wrist in his left hand and she froze. With his unoccupied hand he'd begun to undo his pants.

'You know I didn't bring you up here to blather on,' he said smugly. 'Shut up and get undressed! You're going to be grateful to me. Very grateful.'

'Am I?' she said, without a flicker of betraying emotion. 'All right, let me have some room, will you? I guess I've nothing to lose.'

Kilkieran gave her a sneer of a smile and let go of her. 'Not your maidenhead, the town gossip goes. Cut the palaver, sweetheart. Do it!'

She crossed to an open space between the dresser and the washstand.

Pretending to have qualms — well, she did have plenty but not of the sort he imagined — she turned her back to him and started to unbutton her blouse.

'Don't be shy,' he warned. 'Peel it off in front of me. I can see you in the mirror anyways.'

Now was the moment to make her move. She swung back, hoisting the full pitcher of water that stood on the washstand. He was tugging his partly opened shirt over his head, displaying a chest as hairy as a black bear's.

It couldn't be better. She dashed the cold water full at him, smashed the pitcher over his head, pushed him — tripping him in the tangle of his unfastened, falling pants — and bolted for the door. All in double-quick time.

'Pleasure you, jackass? You must be outa your mind!' she flung.

'Damn you, bitch!' he spluttered. 'You'll regret this — you see if you don't!'

*   *   *

Had the Preacher's talk of an expedition into the hills and mountains been just a come-on line? Lil decided it had. In the days after she'd cooled his ardour for him, he gave her a wide berth, except in the restaurant where he gave his orders as usual but otherwise limited himself to the odd smart, cutting comment.

He switched his attentions to another of the waitresses, Estelle. She was a naive and fragile beauty with no great worldly experience who surely didn't share Lil's singular abilities as a frontierswoman.

Albeit that they were completely different in character, Lil counted Estelle the best friend she'd made among the girls at Ma Coutts's hotel. She watched developments with dismay. She had a suspicion Kilkieran was working up to taking advantage of Estelle as a retaliation against herself.

On returning to the hotel after the gala, she was amazed to learn that he'd stood by apparently unmoved by the robbing of the bank and the gunning-down of innocent citizens on the street.

His boastful talk of an earlier life adventurously roaming the wildest territories of the West, his holier-than-thou term as a Catholic priest, his high-sounding record as the benevolent businessman who'd set up a resort for the cure and comfort of the unhealthy . . . it all surely came to a steaming heap of bullshit when you stacked it up against what he'd done that afternoon: a fat nothing.

Which made his renewed obnoxious-ness all the more puzzling. Sit on his knee indeed!

Previously, she'd thwarted his pre-sumptuous notion that she'd let him have his way with her and accompany him on his research trips. Now, he was surely shamed in many others' eyes, too. Yet here he was wisecracking and teasing her as badly as ever. The starch she'd taken out of him seemed to have been put back in again since the rob-bery. What had restored his humour?

Of course, he'd given his reassurances to the ineffective Sheriff Hamish Howard.

Howard had fronted up with his new tin badge glinting on his pride-strained leather vest. He was a big man, running to fat, with a small, thin-lipped mouth between flabby jowls.

'This is a mighty bad business, Mr Kilkieran, an' I don't know how we're gonna clean it up.' (The sorry excuse for a sheriff had made no attempt to raise a posse and ride after the bank bandits.) 'What were you doin' at the time?'

'Watching, Sheriff,' Kilkieran said drily. 'I saw it from my balcony. There was nothing else a man of peace could do, that's for damn sure. I've not been a shootist in a coon's age. Never a lawman.'

'Can you put a name to any o' the murderin' skunks?'

Kilkieran spread his hands. 'I'm a stranger in the territory. I'd never seen any of their faces before. They were mean *hombres* I wouldn't want to tangle with.'

Howard meekly accepted his unhelpful protestations and stumped off, sighing and mumbling about it being a pity no real fighting men had been in town.

Cowards, both of them, Lil thought. Howard hadn't the guts to go up against ruthless criminals. And Kilkieran . . . No, on second thoughts he was no coward. He was of tougher mettle than he made out. His behaviour hadn't been fitting for a man with his chequered past record and ready to go up against wilderness, winter, and savage redmen to seek a town site.

Not even as a witness had he told Sheriff Howard anything worth a damn.

Lil felt ill-at-ease. What was Preacher Kilkieran up to? She put it in her mind to find out, convinced the man was as tricky and dangerous as a coiled snake.

4

BACKYARD DEAL

The Silver Vein citizenry, like Sheriff Howard and perhaps with greater justification, decided fast enough that tracking the bank robbers was none of their affair. The town, after all, was built close to outlaw country which drew wanted men like a magnet. The vicinity already had a history as a haunt of ranchers and rustlers, miners and claim jumpers.

Folks tutted, accepted the bank's losses philosophically and returned to their everyday business. The gala-day raid became yesterday's stale news.

Misfit Lil complained, 'There's been too damned much killing and robbing in these parts. It ought to be tamed.'

Ma Coutts, who took a motherly interest in her girls, having no family of her own, tried to calm her indignation.

'What you don't understand is that there'll always be bunches of wild men in this area who'd rather thieve and fight than work for honest money. Many big men, too, rustled theirselves a nice start in the cattle business. So they ain't interfering today. Set a thief to catch a thief don't make sense.'

Lil nodded, her face set in thoughtful lines. 'Yes,' she said slowly. 'That's true, Ma, of course.'

'Figure on the Outlaw Trail thing — a gent can travel from Canada to Mexico on it and be let alone. He can raid horse herds and cattle and move them along easy. It hurts the ranchers, but because they've done their own wild things in the past, they let it alone.'

'This wasn't cows — it was a bank raid,' Lil objected.

'Fellers tire of stealing small bunches of critters and collecting the stuff to make a good-sized trail herd,' Ma said, in the manner of a matriarch handing down her wisdom. 'When the chance offers, they use their brains and turn to banks, I guess.'

Lil didn't persist. None of what Ma Coutts was telling her was new. Her father was Ben Goodnight, owner of the biggest spread around, the Flying G. She'd grown up with outlaw stories. She knew better than Ma Coutts about 'inaccessible' hideouts in desolate places where lawmen brave or foolish enough to venture got lost in the mazes of dried-up gullies and box canyons, to meet death from thirst or by a drygulcher's bullet.

She also knew her father, a pillar of local society, had a murky back trail, as many did.

Yet she listened respectfully, wondering instead about Ma's own past. She let her curious eyes stray to the old framed picture on the sideboard in Ma's private parlour — a young boy, a child, with flaxen curls. Lil herself hadn't been bold enough yet to enquire about this portrait, so plainly treasured by a spinster lady. Rumour had it the boy was at the very heart of the hotel landlady's secret sorrow — a bastard son stolen away as an infant by his scoundrel father, now long dead.

'You've a place here now at the Traveller's Hotel, Lil,' Ma Coutts finished up. 'Don't concern yourself with the bank killings. It's too awful for a young woman to fret about.'

So Lil, like everybody else, put the images of Moses Goldberg, P.J. Richardson and Eddie Chaney lying in pools of blood out of her mind.

She wasn't so successful in ignoring the enigma of Patrick 'Preacher' Kilkieran.

In particular, Lil was worried about his seduction of pretty Estelle, who confessed she was an unsophisticated girl who didn't possess the arts to deny him his way with her.

'He's not *nice*, I suppose, but he's such a knowing, mature man,' she said in a voice tinged with awe. 'And very rich and important, they do say. It feels foolish trying to deter him.'

Lil gave up on hoping she could instil

Estelle with the backbone to cope with Kilkieran; it was her private problem at the end of the day. But she didn't give up on spying on Kilkieran's other activities as much as she could.

Convinced he was full of wickedness, a no-good sonofabitch, she resolved to expose the error of his ways to the larger world. It was her commitment to this that found her on hand to be an unseen audience to an odd meeting.

On Saturday night, supper was served promptly so Ma's girls could finish early, dress up in their best clothes and slip away to the local dance, held in a hump-roofed barn at the edge of town called, rather grandly, the Hall.

Lil could enjoy the music — the scrape of the fiddle, the twang of the guitar and the reedy wail of the accordion — but she didn't have a beau, and powder, paint and frilly petticoats were definitely not her style. The one real attraction was that sometimes Jackson Farraday went along.

Dawdling in her cubicle of a room

when all the other waitresses had left, Lil heard a soft and stealthy tread on the back stairs from the guests' upper quarters. A creak and a muted curse.

She peeped out. The identity of the man sidling along the passageway, past the empty kitchen and to the rear door was too shadowy to make out at first, but when he eased open the door the dim illumination of a small lamp burning on its wall-bracket on the porch showed her it was Preacher Kilkieran.

He let himself out, cat-footed, into the little yard back of the hotel.

Lil glided to the door after him. He'd left it ajar, but to follow would be to show herself. She peered round the door's edge cautiously.

It was almost full dark outside, but the weak light of the porch lamp that would betray her presence if she stepped further also sufficed to show Kilkieran moving across the yard to the gate in the high fence.

He unlatched and opened it and

checked the alley outside, looking long and searchingly toward its mouth. He drew his expensive gold timepiece from his vest and flipped open the hinged cover.

With a grunt, he shifted back into the yard and stood with his back against the fence a few paces from the gate.

Lil formed the idea he was expecting to meet someone. She debated making a dash for the cover of an outhouse which stood in the yard, but she'd still likely be as many paces from Kilkieran and the gate as she was now and the risk of being seen outweighed the possible benefit.

Minutes passed and the darkness steadily deepened. Kilkieran was un-moving as a statue, almost lost in the inky-black shadow of the high fence.

Finally, Lil's ears caught the faintest of sounds. She tensed, every nerve and muscle on the alert. Resolved as she was to get to the bottom of the Kilkieran mystery, she felt the beat of her heart quicken with excitement. Was she about to get her answers?

The scuff of a soft, muffled tread reached her. Someone was approaching secretively along the back alley. An exultant grin came to her lips.

Sly to the last moment, Kilkieran, who must have also heard the apparent prowler, kept to his post. But when the figure approached the entry along the other side of the fence, he stepped forward and addressed the arrival in a low voice.

Lil strained to make out words but was unsuccessful. The surprise was delivered by her eyes. The figure that loomed through the open gateway was of an Indian.

The Indian moved forward another step into the yard and halted. He responded with a grunt to the lurking white man who'd quietly accosted him.

He looked by the light of the rising moon like a reservation Apache. He wore a crumpled, highcrowned hat and had a blanket over shoulders clad in a tatty sheepskin vest and a calico shirt.

The shirt's tails hung down over a breechclout and high leggings and moccasins.

The odd pair exchanged more words; Kilkieran sibilant, the Indian guttural so that Lil could make out none of the substance of their conversation.

' . . . stories prove nothing, but mebbe you try . . . ' the Indian said.

' . . . can certainly do my damnedest . . . ' Kilkieran said.

Amid further mutterings, the pair exchanged a grave handshake, as though to seal a deal. Then the Apache slipped away into the dark alley, as softly as he'd come.

Kilkieran started back toward the hotel. Lil knew she was going to learn no more, that the little she'd seen and heard was puzzling and frustrating, but to be caught eavesdropping on the loathsome Preacher was no part of her intentions.

She ducked back to her room, closing the door only moments before Kilkieran ghosted past and slunk up the stairs.

The squeak of a loose plank in the third tread confirmed his progress.

Lil felt an urgent need to discuss her discoveries.

Sheriff Howard was out of the question. At best, he'd scoff; at worst, he'd laugh. The ol' coot hadn't learned much yet about lawdogging, except how to stay out of trouble (Sheriff *Coward*), deny others a voice, and gather the fees and taxes that were the due of his office.

Jackson Farraday was the most obvious man to consult in Lil's prejudiced opinion. Aside from his general knowledge of Indians and their affairs, she had a specific reason to put to him the story of what she'd witnessed.

She threw a cloak over her unloved work clothes and a shawl over her head and headed for the town dance where she hoped Jackson would be.

The musicians were playing feverishly and the dance caller was in full cry. A townswoman sat at the door of the hall by a table stacked with divested outer clothing.

'You can leave your cloak here,' she said and, seeing it was Misfit Lil, 'also your firearms, if'n you're heeled.'

Lil shook her head and went straight by, leaving the doorkeeper gape-mouthed.

She blinked under the light of the many lamps hanging from the rafters between coloured paper streamers. On the floor were five sets of square dancers, the men circling the ladies a'heel an' toeing. 'Swing 'em, kiss 'em if you can!' the caller sing-songed.

Jackson Farraday was sitting out, as was his wont, drinking a beer on the row of benches flanking the right wall, watching the swirl of the skirts. Lil went straight to him.

'Why, Miss Lilian, this is a pleasure — '

'I need to speak with you, Jackson,' she broke in.

The band on the raised platform, led by a whiskery German miner squeezing an accordion, was coming stridently to the last bars of the square dance.

'Talking we can't do here,' Jackson said. 'Mebbe some other time . . . '

'No, now!' Lil said.

Frowning at her persistence and noting the urgency in her voice, he said, 'Well, all right.'

He came to his feet, uncoiling his powerful frame smoothly, and followed her to a side door that gave out on to a cottonwood-shaded corral. The place was more commonly used by the dancers for intercourse other than earnest consultations, but no couples were out there at present.

Lil let her story tumble out. 'He's up to no good, I'm sure. That story of looking for mineral springs is a crock of stinkwater! Can you think of such a thing in this territory?'

Jackson stroked his chin, his eyes twinkling at her flushed excitement.

'Not right off, but Pagosa Springs ain't too far off — across the border and fifty some miles west of Durango in south-western Colorado.'

Inside the barn, the musicians had

struck up with the *Blue Danube* waltz, which might explain the continued absence of courting couples outside. The lilting sentimentality of the music, led by the plaintive accordion, tugged at Lil's heartstrings. Being alone in this setting with the handsome, mature . . . *untouchable* Jackson was an experience she found very unsettling, but she couldn't put aside her mission to indulge foolish feelings.

She came close to a hurt pout. 'You think Kilkieran's on the level with his resort-site story?'

'Pagosa is Ute for Healing Waters,' said Jackson. 'That place's known real well. The Navajos challenged the Utes for possession for centuries, and that's a fact. In 1866, the Utes agreed ownership of it could be decided by single combat. They chose for their man Henry Pfeiffer, a transplanted Scot who'd worked alongside Kit Carson and been an Indian agent. He threw his Bowie knife at his Navajo rival, killing him.'

'Hmm! Very interesting,' Lil said, with a measure of sarcasm, because she was young enough not to like being found wrong by a man she wanted to impress. 'But for why should Kilkieran be having a secret meeting with an Indian?'

'Could be an innocent reason. These days some Indians do business reg'lar with white men.'

'Not in the dark! Not this white man, and not this Indian!'

'What do you mean?'

Lil produced her trump card. 'I don't believe the Indian was off the reservation. I seem to recall I seen his face someplace else.'

'All right. Long as this ain't just crazy talk — where? And why is it so all-fired important?'

'D'you recollect the attack on the army paymaster's wagon by Angry-fist and his renegades?'

'How could I forget, or your part in it?' He shook his head and laughed softly, wonderingly. 'Lieutenant Covington fired me over that fiasco.'

Lil stared hard into Jackson's blue-grey eyes. 'I reckon Kilkieran's Indian was one of the bunch who rode with Angry-fist.'

Jackson pondered. 'All right. So what do we do with this hunch you've gotten about a rebel Indian you think you recognized in the dark?'

Lil understood his point. 'I don't know. It beats the hell out of me. That's why I've told you.'

'It's Kilkieran really, ain't it? You don't like him.'

'No, I don't. He hasn't a lick of respect and was set on forcing himself on me. Now he's sweethearting Estelle and the poor girl don't know how to say no. He's playing her for a sucker to spite me, but I'll get even with him somehow.'

'I sympathize, Miss Lilian. He sounds lower than a snake's belly, but right now it's like you s'pose — the county ain't going to be interested, and it's nothing a body could put to the territorial governor or the military. I don't think there's a thing you can or should do.'

The waltz in the barn came to its finish in a climax, followed by a patter of handclapping and joyful exclamations.

5

CRUEL PUNISHMENT

Patrick Kilkieran's plans were proceeding apace. Disregarding winter's imminence, he figured it high time to act on his desire to depart the dubious hospitality of Silver Vein.

It would have been a bonus to have a guide to take him the next step of the journey, but it wasn't to be. The professional scout Jackson Farraday was too straight and too savvy for what he had in mind. The best alternative, young Lilian Goodnight, would have made a satisfying bonus, sharing his blankets on the trail, but she'd let him know what she thought of him in no uncertain terms.

Before he quit this two-bit town, he was going to pay the bitch back for that. And he could do the job through her friend and workmate, Estelle.

When it came to having a woman, Estelle had pleased him as a substitute for Lil. Her seduction was more fulfilling than any sleazy, quick and costly encounters with out-and-out whores. Yet the girl was good for nothing much else — not, for sure, a trek into the wilderness.

She was a pretty little wench, very blonde, with quiet blue eyes and delicate skin as smooth as the finest silk under his exploring fingertips. Fortunately for the needful male, she hadn't learned the irritating female art of striking a balance between acquiescence and refusal. He'd feasted his jaded appetites, taking liberties that had embarrassed the she-noodle.

Kilkieran relished that Lil knew Estelle had given what she'd denied him. She'd advised Estelle not to yield, and was angry about his victory. If looks could kill, Lil's would. As a parting shot, he would do something totally degrading to Estelle that would •

leave Lil seething and impotent to retaliate. She'd know then forever that he'd had the real power and she'd had none, despite her famed shooting ability to hit the eye of a bird flying in the air.

Oh, yes, Kilkieran thought, Estelle might be no good for the longer trail, but having had his fill of her vulnerable beauty, he could now use it as a weapon to fix Misfit Lil.

When Estelle came to his room on what he planned to make his last night at the Traveller's Hotel, Kilkieran cajoled her into staying well into the early hours of the morning. He put her through the repertoire of his warped fancies, and was more than usually rough with her, but when he made his new, ultimate demand, she found the courage to say no.

They had been drinking champagne copiously, but Estelle was not so befuddled as not to recognize what he wanted to witness was beyond the bounds of all ordinary pleasures of the flesh.

'Are you mad? I'm not going there to do that. It's — unnatural, impossible! A girl would be killed . . . '

He gave an ugly laugh. He knew what she said was right and he'd bargained on her answer.

'You'll come to the livery with me anyways. I've paid the night hostler to make hisself scarce and gotten it all set up.'

Estelle jumped up from his bed. It would have been an impressive flounce if she'd been wearing more than a thin shift.

'What do you mean?'

'I mean, jade, since you ain't willing, you'll pay for it with punishment that'll teach you a lesson — you and your uppity pal Misfit Lil both.'

He lunged after her. He seized her round her slim waist and twisted a kerchief round her face.

'Stop it! I — !' she blurted, but the rest was smothered. The dry cloth went into her open mouth, gagging her, and though she beat furiously at his strong arms, her puny blows were ineffective.

Fear filled her wide, bright blue eyes.

He flung her down on the bed, and slapped her face, knocking resistance out of her. With contemptuous ease, he rolled her over, and jerked her arms behind her to pinion her wrists with a leather string. He caught her drumming feet and dealt with them similarly.

'Woman, am I going to enjoy this!' he growled.

He hoisted her light form over his shoulder and left his room, heading for the back stairs.

★ ★ ★

Misfit Lil stirred in her sleep. A faint noise had percolated her dormant senses. She raised her head from the pillow and listened. Had she heard the creak of the back stairs, the lift of the back door's latch?

No, it was probably just her subconscious rerunning the episode of

Kilkieran meeting the Indian.

Pillows! A head could be rested better on a saddle . . . She plumped it and snuggled back down under the sheets.

★ ★ ★

Kilkieran hauled the gagged girl through the dark toward the glow of the hurricane lamp that lit the doors and runway of the livery barn. She was trying to scream, but the sounds that came out were breathy grunts — urgent but largely inaudible — and served only to sharpen his anticipation.

He lowered her to the ground and dragged her into the shaded gloom of the stables. The stalls to either side being mostly occupied, the place had animal warmth and smell. Kilkieran had observed during a life of considerable diversity that stables had a strong effect on young women not intimately familiar with them. They were an intensely masculine environment. In the messiest, the pungent odours of equine sweat, urine and manure were overpowering.

As part of his preparations for what was to follow, Kilkieran had described to Estelle in detail the attributes of the big black stallion in the end stall. He dumped her on the dirty straw where she could have a good view of this mean animal with his flicking ears and wicked eyes. Though a tractable beast, in the lamplight his largeness alone would appear grossly menacing to a girl already frightened by lewd but ultimately impractical suggestions.

Estelle shook her head vigorously. No, no, she tried to cry, but it came out through the gag as 'Uhmm! Uhmm!'

The night hostler appeared from the harness room — and saw the gagged, bound and scantily covered girl.

'Lord's sakes, Mistuh Kilkieran — '

'Thought I'd paid you to be someplace else, boy,' Kilkieran said. 'Go on — git, scat!'

The hostler's eyes rolled in his head.

'Yessuh, mistuh man! I seen nothin', heard nothin'!'

He scampered away, clutching a bottle that had once held liniment but had been replenished with other potent liquor.

Kilkieran laughed evilly. 'Nope,' he told the girl. 'I don't think Satan here would perform, if I could spreadeagle you over a high enough heap of the right-scented bales. So we'll whip you instead. Call it deserts for ingratitude — for refusing to countenance the notion — for being pally with that pesky Misfit Lil. She'll be plenty sore when she sees it . . . why, maybe as sore as your ownself!'

The straw crunched under his boots as he lifted Estelle under her arms and pulled her toward the harness room. He kicked open the door and took her in.

Between the racks of oiled and polished leather was an open space under a convenient beam. He tossed a rope over the beam, ran it through the loop of her arms, still lashed together at the wrists, and hauled her up.

He was satisfied only when her toes barely touched the floor and her torso was stretched and arced, the lower part of her ribcage conspicuous through the thinness of her shift.

The Preacher chuckled. He chose his weapon — a buggy whip that lay on a workbench. Its stiff handle was split but the four-foot lash of tough, use-darkened rawhide was intact and pliant.

He cracked the whip at his victim's heels.

The suspended girl swayed as she tied to pull herself clear on her arms and made sounds of distress.

Kilkieran decided that, enclosed by the walls of the stable, he could chance enjoying her cries. He reached up and tugged free the gag.

Estelle cried, 'No, you're mad! Mercy, let me down!'

'No mercy, whore . . . till I've whipped the devils of temptation out of your pretty little ass!'

Kilkieran told himself that all men who exposed Estelle's delectable body in the future would see how she'd been marked up. They'd know she was coarsened by her treatment; that healthy, youthful responses to normal physical attentions would have been vitiated before their time. A man liked to fool himself he was the first. He didn't need to be reminded he wasn't by the blatant scars of another's abuse.

The first stinging crack of the whip tore a scream from his victim's dry throat; the second, a choking moan and, from her pale white body, a shred of the shift that curled around the whip end and flapped like a piece of bunting. The third sweeping cut broke the girl's delicate skin and pitched her into a disappointing semi-consciousness.

Kilkieran turned his fiendish energies to producing a symmetrical pattern of red weals.

★　★　★

Misfit Lil was roused again. From a distance had come a cry, like of pain. Coyotes out in the wild? No, it had been closer than that, she was sure, somewhere in the township itself. A shrill sound, but deadened by its passage through lumber, stone and brick.

Puzzled, curious and a mite alarmed, she got off her cot. She remembered the sounds she thought she'd heard of someone using the back stairs again, and thought of Kilkieran and his mysterious behaviour.

She pulled on clothes — not her waitress's blouse and skirt, but pants and buckskin shirt. She buckled the gunbelt around her hips and snuck out. First she scooted upstairs. Doubts dissolved as she saw Kilkieran's door was ajar. Looking in, a quick check showed the room empty, though the bed had apparently been vigorously used, with the covers and sheets in a heap on the floor. A struggle?

Lil thought of Estelle; remembered

the muffled scream.

Downstairs again, she found the rear door unbolted. She went out quickly, but was uncertain which way to turn when she reached the yard gate and found that, too, wasn't secured.

She went through the alley and on to Main Street. A droning and the clink of a bottle drew her attention to a slumped shape under the steps up to the plank walk by the late Moses Goldberg's store. It was Sam, the boy who was supposed to look after the livery barn nights. He was slurring and humming a bastardized version of a spiritual; he was drunk out of his brain.

Lil then heard inexplicable sounds coming from the barn. They weren't the kind resting horses made. She stepped out, again swiftly but cautiously, for the place.

Unmistakably, as she approached, she made out the crack of a whip, followed by a low moan and a grunt that may have been a snigger of approval. It came to her in a flash of realization what might be happening and the probable identities of the actors. She felt a chill of horror and anger run through her.

'I'll kill the louse!' she swore.

It was just possible Estelle had accompanied the Preacher to the stables of her own free will, but no girl would have elected to submit to the ordeal Lil was hearing. She could face irretrievable ruin.

Lil burst into the stables at a silent run, drawing her guns from their holsters, cocking the right weapon as it cleared leather.

The scene that confronted her in the harness room was as ugly as anything she'd imagined. Estelle was strung from a beam, barely conscious, her shift in tatters and her back fiercely splotched and welted.

Kilkieran flourished a buggy whip. He whirled with a snarl of fury as he realized he'd been discovered at his foul work.

'Who the hell — ?'

Maybe Lil should then have followed her first resolve — to shoot Patrick Kilkieran dead on sight. But she was reminded at the crucial moment he was a man of some celebrity. He had a silver tongue. At a guess, he might have spun some convincing yarn about her and Estelle and this bizarre set-up. Her own reputation wasn't good. Folks believed anything about Misfit Lil; putting a hangrope around her neck to ease the pains in their butts would appeal to many she could name, of either gender. So she levelled the right gun and squeezed the trigger to terminate Estelle's ordeal.

The gun slammed against Lil's palm. The shot crashed out, flame leaping from the muzzle. Her accuracy was perfect as ever, despite the split-second speed with which she'd deliberated over and reacted to the harrowing sight; the less than ideal lamplight.

The whip was hurled from Kilkieran's grasp, its split handle now shattered by the .45 slug. But Kilkieran was a fighter from way back who'd been in tight spots before this. He ducked behind a solid bench stacked with saddles and whipped a revolver of his own from a shoulder holster. A blur of motion, he fired right back . . .

Missed.

Lil retreated to the door. Would he miss if she showed herself again? She'd never been in a more nightmarish predicament.

The echoes of the gun cracks died within the harness-room. Grey gun-smoke swirled. Outside, several horses stomped restively.

'You're cornered, Kilkieran,' she bluffed. 'Throw out your piece and come on out real slow. We're taking this to Sheriff Howard.'

Kilkieran had other ideas. 'Don't count on it, missy. The fool don't figure on any calling list of mine.'

'I'll take you to the sheriff's office at gunpoint if I have to.'

Kilkieran jeered, 'How long do you think that's going to take — raising the sheriff and all, supposing it goes down as you say?'

Lil knew the answer. With Estelle badly abused, too long. She didn't cotton to the idea of admitting she held a weak hand. She said nothing.

'This here's a standoff,' Kilkieran said. 'Someone's got to cut down your pal soon, and I'm damned if it'll be me with you waving guns around. You let me out of here and you can get on with tending her. Course, if you want to make a gunfight of it, that's your prerogative, I guess. No guarantee Estelle won't catch stray lead if you do.'

Estelle was coming round. She moaned and whimpered, then began crying like a child at the horrible agony of her raw, bleeding body.

Misfit Lil decided. 'All right. I'm coming in and you can come on out. But remember this, I'm no slouch with a pistol.'

She thumbed back the hammers of both Colts and edged into the room.

6

THE UNLOVING WIFE

'I'll be coming after you, you bastard — that's a promise,' Lil said.

With guns drawn, she and the Preacher circled round the unfortunate girl, strung on her stretched arms from the harness-room beam. They were like cats, claws out and spitting, daring one another to begin a scrap.

Kilkieran was full of scorn and bravado. 'You'll do nothing to cross me — '

'Listen to me!' Lil flared. 'I'm not staking my life or Estelle's right now. But this here's enough to put you away — ten years' hard by my reckoning — if'n I don't get the chance to kill you.'

'You kid yourself, bitch! Drop it — we've nothing more to talk about.'

Bitterly, Lil had to watch as he backed out of the stables, with the hateful curl of a sneer still on his lips.

She wasted no time once he'd left. She'd let him go and the consequences of that couldn't be altered for the moment. Estelle's very life might depend on how fast she acted.

She took a knife to the taut rope securing her to the beam. It was too taut, the knots pulled too tight by her sufferings, to untie. Estelle had no strength left in her and fell into her arms, the pain of contact wrenching a weak cry from her trembling lips.

Lil lowered her to the floor and met her eyes. She would remember ever after the black anguish she saw in them.

'Oh, help me, Lil,' Estelle gasped pitifully. 'I've been such a poor damned fool.'

Lil looked for and found a blanket that was passably clean and wrapped Estelle in it. 'I'm strong for a girl,' she assured her. 'I can carry you back to the hotel where we'll be able to clean you up.'

By the time the burdened Lil had reached the hotel, Estelle had lapsed into a semi-coma of shock again. Lil opened the huge cast-iron cookstove in the kitchen, pokered the banked-up fire and threw kindling on to the previous day's smouldering embers. She needed hot water to soak the remnants of Estelle's shift off her ravaged back. She filled a kettle from a water pitcher. If she moved fast, maybe she could lift the tatters from the poor cut, blood-clotted back and apply some salve and bandages before Estelle woke up. It was going to be hell for her; some shreds of fabric appeared actually mingled with the flesh.

Lil quivered with suppressed emotion. 'The skunk's not fit to live,' she muttered. 'The only way anyone'll ever get even with Preacher Kilkieran is by killing him.'

Come first light, Lil had Estelle resting, sure to survive the horrible episode, but feverish and uncomfortable. Sipping a cup of hot, sweet tea, Estelle begged Lil not to make known what she saw as the dues of her folly — just to say she was sick. She didn't want any doctor or nurse calling either.

'But it was barbaric — despicable!' Lil protested. 'It's no girl's needings to be used so.'

Whatever spark of fight Estelle had had in her had been beaten out.

'People like to talk — Lord, don't they love to talk? They'd say I had it coming.'

Reluctantly, Lil let her have her way. Besides, another development made a quick and public reckoning doubly impractical. Kilkieran didn't show in the hotel restaurant for breakfast. Lil checked in on his room and found it emptied of the man and his possessions.

'He lit out right early on his lonesome,' Ma Coutts told her. 'Should it be anything to you?'

'Where's he gone?'

'How should I know? Mebbe off a-hunting townsite prospects in the mountains. Looking for salubrious hot springs like the Mormons bathe in at Salt Lake City. That's what he talked of, wasn't it?'

Lil's brow furrowed. 'He must be crazy heading out into country he doesn't know. It's the wrong season.'

Outside, it was growing cold and the promise of winter's first snow had turned to threat. It would already be falling in the mountains. Was Kilkieran such a tenderfoot as to head deep into the towering wastes without the proper supplies and a guide?

Lil thought she knew damned well why Kilkieran had lit a shuck, of course. She said no more to her boss, but went to confirm some suspicions.

From Moses Goldberg's son, Ike, she learned that Kilkieran had just yesterday bought essential comestibles in 'considerable' amounts: flour, salt, baking-powder, coffee, sugar, plus tobacco, matches and, puzzlingly, two jugs of whiskey of the rotgut variety sold illegally to the Indians. At the livery barn she found out more. Kilkieran had recently bought a string of three horses and had set out with them heavily laden with packs he'd brought to the barn from Goldberg's place.

The sky was grey and the air still and dead as her cold thoughts as Lil hurried next to the boarding house where Jackson Farraday lodged between his scouting assignments. She was relieved to find he hadn't been hired by Patrick Kilkieran.

A familiar, strangely soundless quality had settled on the town, but the words spilled out of Lil in a wild tumble. She confided in Jackson completely, knowing she could trust him.

'I've got to go after him,' she said, resolute that Kilkieran should answer for his conduct.

Jackson was grave, disturbed, but measured in his response.

'You can't do it, Miss Lilian. You're under a bond to Ma Coutts, aren't you?

That won't be served out till spring. And you know if your pa were to hear of your plan, he'd likely act to prevent it.'

'Only because he wouldn't want a Goodnight upsetting a rich Colorado landowner!'

'Be that as maybe, or maybe not, there's not a thing you can do anyhow. Look . . . the snow's begun. Kilkieran's tracks'll be covered. It'd take weeks to find him, if you ever did.'

Lil groaned. Like she'd known it would, snow was drifting down in its first, small scattered flakes. Over the next half-hour it would surely thicken. If the wind picked up, it would turn into a real blizzard that would curtail movement in and out of the area indefinitely.

'A trail hidden by falling snow is a trail lost forever,' she said.

'Afraid so,' her mentor said.

★　★　★

Despite best endeavours and all discretion, word eventually leaked out about 'a private incident' between two of Ma's Girls and the guest who'd disappeared into inhospitable country at the start of winter.

But universally, it seemed to Lil, Silver Vein shrugged its uncaring shoulders. The untamed West was a man's world. Society was conscienceless and altogether nasty, regardless of its claims to chivalry and opportunity. 'The hell with all loose women! Good riddance to spendthrift adventurers with loco get-rich schemes!' And Misfit Lil was widely said to be the most meddling, pernicious, immodest female anyone could be cursed to meet.

Successive storms laid a throttling grip on the land; winter was king everywhere. A search for a man who failed to return was nobody's business, Lil was told. Hope of rescue or retribution was pure delusion. If the elements hadn't done for Patrick Kilkieran, then hostile Indians would.

Lil vowed repeatedly, but refrained from openly declaring, that come spring she'd get even with the vicious and foolhardy Preacher, if he still lived.

Winter did indeed pass with no sign of or word from the man from Pure Waters Colony, Colorado. A popular rumour was he'd survived the first storm but fallen foul of Angry-fist's renegades.

The next significant development coincided with the melting of the snows and a change in the weather to typical springtime unpredictability — wet and windy one day, sunny and calm the next.

The stage rattled into Silver Vein on a fine March day and rolled to its customary stop, which was right in front of the Traveller's Hotel. The whip dropped the lines and applied the brake. He clambered down from his high perch on the box and ran to open the coach door.

Lil stayed at the window of the hotel restaurant for some moments, watching the driver offer his hand to the woman who stepped from the stage. He was very attentive and rushed to unload her carpet bag. The arrival was plainly a woman of substance, over-dressed for travel. The flounced skirts under her tailored top coat must have taken up most of one seat of the coach, and she wore a ridiculous feathered hat where a snug-fitting bonnet would have been more appropriate.

The woman straightened the hat and said something in wrathful tones to the driver, probably about the rigours of her journey.

The pair came into the hotel, the driver toting her bag.

'You can fix yourself up soon enough now,' he said. 'And they'll be delighted to serve you some food. And coffee, eh, Mrs Kilkieran?'

Kilkieran!

Lil's ears pricked up with intense interest. Was the arrival Patrick Kilkieran's *wife*? If so, could she shed light on her husband's present whereabouts? Was he returning here to meet her?

Lil's heart leaped and she had to work at controlling her excitement. The name and the woman's presence might be matters of coincidence after all, she told herself. She could be a mere relative by marriage, passing through.

It transpired Mrs Blanche Kilkieran brought neither a breakthrough nor an end to Lil's resolve to find the Preacher and bring him to account.

Mrs Kilkieran was not exactly willing to discuss her business with a waitress, but Lil was able to piece together the story via Ma Coutts and other sources of town news. Blanche Kilkieran was at as big a loss as anyone to explain the disappearance of her spouse, who was indeed Patrick Kilkieran.

'She can't believe he's dead,' Ma Coutts divulged. 'The poor woman's distraught . . . You'll keep this to yourself, won't you?'

'Sure, Ma.'

The face of the hotel proprietress became grave. 'It's a terrible thing to be deprived of one close to your heart.'

Her watery gaze wandered to the picture of the boy on the sideboard.

Lil hadn't been particularly aware of Blanche Kilkieran's distress. She ate heartily at mealtimes, having a taste for thick slices of beef steak, done at her loud insistence medium rare. Lil had also overheard her conversations with other guests.

Blanche confided in a rather handsome drummer that the Pure Waters Colony in Colorado was being brought to a 'parlous state' by the continued absence of its charismatic founder and his legendary healing powers.

She patted her blonde coiffure — which Lil thought owed much to the application of peroxide — and complained of cancelled bookings and lost revenue.

'You know, I had to divorce my first husband, who was a milliner in New York, on account of his strayings. When I hitched up with Patrick it was because I knew I could supply the business smartness to turn his health colony into a thriving resort and bathing place. I made it somewhere, too, that the wealthy could indulge in genteel sport and gambling — cardplaying, horse-backing and the like — for decent stakes, with only a small percentage going to the house, of course.'

The smarmy drummer said, 'I'm sure you made Mr Kilkieran's marital life a good one.'

Lil got a different picture. Blanche was a hard woman in a town-ish way. She reckoned her heart was a stone and if she was distraught, like Ma Coutts said, it was over the threat to her own comfortable circumstances.

Though young, Lil was shrewd enough to reckon marriage between Kilkieran and Blanche couldn't have been any bed of roses. He had his passing enthusiasms, as evidenced by his chequered career; she was a woman who pursued her ambitions single-mindedly. Not a love-match, Lil thought.

Nor was it concern for Kilkieran's well-being and safety that brought

Blanche here now. She wanted to restore the connubial fortunes. Everything else was a blind.

Well, if Blanche was anxious to track down Kilkieran, so was she. Though they had vastly different reasons, that gave them a shared interest, though the woman was someone for whom Lil would never have sisterly feelings.

With her time at the Traveller's Hotel about served out, Lil took the bull by the horns — if such a metaphor could be applied to one so brittle and fashionably attired — and approached Blanche.

'I understand you're here to look for your husband, Mrs Kilkieran. Could I be so bold as to suggest I could work for you as a guide? I might look no more'n a serving girl to you, but I've a good name for knowing this country, being born and raised in it. I'm also as good a tracker as an Indian. The army scout Jackson Farraday will vouch for my skills, and he's the very best.'

Blanche looked at her as though she

was a slug that had crawled out of her salad.

'I think not, young woman,' she said, incredulous. 'Plainly you've been listening to talk about me and my affairs. Well, so have I — about you and your mousy little colleague.'

'Oh?'

Lil near busted herself holding her tongue to the monosyllabic response while also aching to deny vehemently that the grievously wronged Estelle could be dismissed as a mouse.

'Indeed.' Blanche lowered her voice. 'Miss Goodnight, you and your pal are both *sluts*, and you'll not pull the wool over my eyes like you did Patrick's — '

'Beg pardon, ma'am, we did no such thing!'

Blanche disregarded the protest and continued in a voice dripping with vituperation. 'I understand Miss Coutts runs no bawdy house, but she's apt to wink at what goes on behind closed doors apparently.'

'Is that so?' Lil said, her voice taking

on a cold undercurrent of anger. 'Huh! When I hear such uncharitable righteousness, I know I'm listening to a hypocrite, ma'am. You can go lose yourself in the canyonlands for all I care. I'll not help you find your husband now if you beg me to. I hope he's dead!'

'I never asked for your help, whore. I've already gone calling to Colonel Brook Lexborough, commanding officer at Fort Dennis — '

'I know who Colonel Lexborough is,' Lil said acidly, wondering what was coming next.

'And the colonel has recommended I should hire your Mr Jackson Farraday himself, not some stripling with ideas above her station!'

'Damn,' Lil said under her breath. 'Damn, damn . . . '

The first damn was for Blanche Kilkieran; the second for Colonel Lexborough; the third for the whole, Misfit Lil-hostile world. She stacked and scooped up Blanche's dirty breakfast dishes with a brisk clatter and retreated.

If she'd been a more normal girl, about now would have been the time to have a case of the vapours. The notion of the masterly and accomplished Jackson Farraday being at the beck and call of this hateful woman, at the mercy of her designs — and Lil was suddenly, jealously sure she had them — made her sick to the stomach.

7

SAVING BLANCHE

When Misfit Lil observed Blanche Kilkieran's preparations, she swiftly if reluctantly rode to the guardhouse at Fort Dennis.

The fort saw a steady stream of civilian visitors of every stripe. Ranchers protested about cattle supposedly rustled by reservation Indians; the Indians complained they were being issued short beef rations by the Indian Bureau's agent; the miners said the Indians denied them access to their claims . . . and so it went on. Colonel Brook Lexborough had an appointment book filled with the names of privilege-seekers, petitioners and cranky time-wasters.

So Lil requested to see Lieutenant Mike Covington. This drew some barely concealed sniggers from the men on duty, since Covington was a darling of the local female population with his smooth and handsome looks and unfailingly immaculate turn-out.

Grudgingly, Lil felt, Covington came to the guardhouse and listened to her appeal.

'Mrs Kilkieran's outfitted herself with fancy range clothes and hired a covered wagon from the livery. They'll be spotted by Angry-fist's band miles off. She'll get herself and Jackson killed, both!'

A strained, exasperated expression came into the young officer's face. 'What do you want me to do, Miss Goodnight?'

'I'm shocked that Colonel Lexborough hasn't warned her off. Angry-fist is out for blood — especially Jackson Farraday's after he lopped off his hand. The colonel should've told her a hunt for her husband was dangerous, imbecile . . . that Preacher Kilkieran's probably been scalped long since.'

'You want me to pass on your concerns to Colonel Lexborough?'

'Yes! No . . . I mean, I want you to ask him to tell Blanche Kilkieran it can't be done.'

Covington said drily, 'I expect he tried, but I'm told Mrs Kilkieran is a very forceful woman.'

'Then the colonel must give them protection — an army escort.'

'Come, Miss Goodnight, Colonel Lexborough can hardly involve the army in a private matter! Washington's latest orders are to go softly on reservation deserters. We don't want an out-and-out war on our hands. The colonel did the best thing in steering Mrs Kilkieran to Jackson Farraday.'

Lil exclaimed in exasperation, 'Do you want Mr Farraday killed?'

'Mr Farraday has always shown himself well able to keep his scalp on. Isn't it really a case of your allowing — uh — personal sentiments to intrude? The army can't be used as a chaperon, you know.'

Covington had witnessed before that, despite the disparity in their ages, Lil Goodnight nursed what he considered an unhealthy adoration for the weather-burnished, trail-hardened scout.

'Oh, you're pathetic, Mike Covington,' Lil groaned.

She was indignant at being let down by Covington, but somehow she'd hardly expected otherwise from the spit-and-polish, ever-obedient graduate of West Point Military Academy.

She abandoned her pleas, muttering about the outrage of official passiveness, and went back to Silver Vein.

Blanche Kilkieran's wagon was in the corral back of the livery barn. It was no prairie schooner of Conestoga size, but with breeze ruffling its white canvas it did look like a small ship about to set sail. The body of the wagon had been painted garter-blue and the running gear was red.

'So the Injuns can see it coming,' Lil observed, quietly and sarcastically, in a bid to lift her sinking spirits.

The wagon, about ten or twelve feet long and four or five wide, was the best Silver Vein could offer. The wheels had three-inch rims, the rear being a foot more in diameter than the front. They were shod with heavy iron tyres, the joints tightly welded, which also helped to keep the wheels together.

The wagon seat was sprung.

Lil peeked inside. Besides space for the storage of supplies, the well contained a bed, unmade, and a fold-down table hinged to the side. At the far end, a tiny cubicle was partitioned off with a bunk for a second sleeper. Lil wondered whether it could accommodate a man of Jackson's physique. Maybe it wouldn't be required to . . .

Lil decided what the situation required of her.

* * *

Jackson Farraday had his doubts about the worth and wisdom of trekking into the bleak hills which had swallowed up

Patrick Kilkieran — a place of sage and stunted cedars and scattered, hard-to-find waterholes. Also to be weighed was the possibility of attack by the hostile Apaches who'd sought sanctuary in the wild and lonely places in preference to the confines of the reservation, where an aspiring warrior was expected to work his treaty-bestowed fields with sober industry.

On the other hand, Jackson was always wont to attach more significance to what he was told by Misfit Lil than he acknowledged to the young woman herself.

He remembered the odd report she'd brought him of the mysterious meeting in the dark backyard of the hotel between Kilkieran and a member of Angry-fist's rebel band. He didn't for one moment think she would have been mistaken in her identification of the Indian. Lil didn't make mistakes — leastways, not of that sort.

Maybe Kilkieran had reached some secret arrangement of safe passage, if not more. It had been something both he and Lil would have liked to check. But the cold, raw winds of winter had come, blowing heavy snow before them, obliterating tracks and isolating the town from all but the nearest flats.

Little, of course, had been heard lately of Angry-fist. He and Misfit Lil had effectively cut off his party's supplies of decent weapons and ammunition by smashing the Boorman's Wells gunrunning operation, and the army, following the policy directions of the Secretary of the Interior, had refrained from harassing the renegades.

Maybe the lull in Apache raids meant the trouble in these parts was over, but Jackson wasn't betting his life on it. He was keeping a sharp eye out as he took Blanche Kilkieran south from Silver Vein on a long, slanting journey into higher hills, away from the stage road and using what were mostly no more than cattle tracks.

He was nagged two ways.

The first was by the prickle at the

back of his neck, the unease in his gut that suggested they were spied on and followed. Such feelings could presage a hail of bullets, though Jackson concluded they wouldn't in this case. They weren't yet in the wildest country where the Apaches and outlaw bands hid out.

He suspected it was Misfit Lil who was dogging them. She'd pulled such stunts on him before. It was part of the infernal, inappropriate interest she took in his doings. He'd tried repeatedly to put a stop to it. He hoped her fascination was a girlish phase she'd grow out of. It embarrassed him, although on occasion he'd had cause to welcome her intrusion into his affairs.

He brought the lurching wagon on to a level, sweeping bench where he could see many miles. He saw no sign of a girl following on a surefooted cow pony. But their back trail was over low rolls in land dotted by thickets of piñon. A line of cottonwoods marked a stream that would eventually tumble into the grim

Colorado River canyons. The cover was scanty but he knew it would be enough for Misfit Lil. She was also advantaged by her ability to take routes impassable by wagon.

The second aggravation was Blanche Kilkieran.

At every jounce of the sprung wagon seat she contrived to lurch against him, sometimes clutching him unnecessarily as though she feared she'd fall from their perch. He was acutely aware that she'd doused herself in a strongly perfumed toilet water. He'd seen the bottle in her bag. Its label declared it Oil of Aphrodite. 'Snake oil more like!' Jackson noted silently. But it did nothing to prevent his awareness of the lush softness of the handsome blonde's full body thrust against him.

He was no ladies' man, had never tried to be such, but away from Silver Vein, Blanche made it plain she wouldn't be averse to more personal service than a guide provided.

'Mr Farraday, may I call you Jackson,

and why don't you drop the Mrs Kilkieran and call me Blanche?'

So it seemed, once she had him to her lonesome and out of folks' sight, they were to be on more companionable terms. When she flung her arms around him at an especially notable lurch of the wagon, cried, 'Save me!' and, in pushing herself off him, let her hand stroke across his belly and tautly stretched pants to his thigh, the die was cast.

'Blanche,' he said with a sigh, 'I'd be a liar if I said I wasn't partial to any saving, but mebbe later there'll be a better time and place.'

He made his suggestion as much as anything else to appease Blanche's ardour, so she might allow him to attend his driving on a difficult route.

But Jackson was, at the end of it all, only human. He did feel a longing, a stirring. Inevitabilities couldn't be turned aside forever, and certainly only with great awkwardness and difficulty when your supper partner, and the only human apparent for miles, decided they shouldn't.

After dining on stew rather than the prime steak, medium rare, she would have relished, Blanche determined she should have her compensation. She rose up and, in the mellow light of the camp-fire, unfastened her dress. She slipped it from her shoulders and let it pool at her ankles.

Jackson felt more than the lick of the fire's heat on his cheeks. His blood was pounding.

'You — uh — don't owe me this,' he said, but not trying overly hard to hide his face in a drained tin coffee cup.

'No,' she confirmed. 'But after that horrible stew, you owe me something filling for dessert. And you said you'd save me. Well, I need saving something fierce — from a powerful hunger, Jackson.' She pulled at a lace and ample globes of flesh spilled free from the restraints of her upper corsetry, which she let fall.

Jackson swallowed at the sight.

Confronted with her strength of will and her unflinching disrobing, it seemed the only practical step to take was to share with her the comfortable bed on the wagon's floor. To sleep under the wagon, or, worse, squeeze his big frame into the bunk in the end cubicle would be ridiculous. Perhaps, too, once he'd given her what she seemed to think she needed, she'd be satisfied and give him some peace.

'I know this will be good for both of us, Jackson,' she said. She swung down the wagon tailgate on its rattling chains, clambered in and leaned out to pull him after her by his left hand.

So he went in and 'saved' her, though from what he wasn't precisely sure. Maybe the demons of an appetite that had been building in her since her husband had left Pure Waters Colony, Colorado. In point of fact, at their first climactic moment, she did hiss in his ear, 'I feel so — abandoned, Jackson!'

Though married to a man who'd once been a skypilot, she seemed not to have heard greed was a further sin. He found her every bit as demanding in bed as she was elsewhere.

Out in the darkness, a coyote called and was answered by the mournful wail of another.

'The cry of the wilderness,' Blanche said, and rolled her smooth, impenitent nakedness on top of his hirsute hardness. 'God, it's so good to be with a man again. Hold me tighter, Jackson.'

He said, jokingly, 'Are you sure those coyotes aren't really prowling Apaches?'

* * *

Misfit Lil had no trouble in following the tracks left by Blanche Kilkieran's wagon. Any difficulty resulted from avoiding skylining herself on bald ridges or standing out on broad flats of sage and bunch grass. Here, concealment was possible only by taking circuitous detours that made full use of the profile of the land.

Late in the day, she lost the wagon

tracks on a section of hard ground after spending considerable time lurking along a stream bed. But she was as sure of her bearings as always, and after casting around, nigh on nightfall she cut sign again.

She located Blanche and Jackson camped in a draw grown with clumps of brush and pines. From a crest, she could see the wagon, now a colourless bulk surmounted by pale canvas; also the silhouettes of man and woman against the dancing flames of a camp-fire. The woman, standing, looked like she was posing. She possessed an enviably full figure.

Lil grunted disgustedly. 'Crazy damned fools . . . like they're on a picnic.'

She retreated to a site where she might camp herself and removed saddle and blankets from her mount. She built a small fire and warmed some food, but not much since she'd no knowing how long her supplies had to last.

Come to that, Lil pondered, what was this jaunt she was on, and when would it be over? When Preacher Kilkieran was found — alive or dead?

After she'd eaten, she pulled out from a saddle-bag a bottle of her favourite bonded whiskey and took two swallows from it which demanded a measure of control greater than the measure of the warming liquor she drank.

Wrapped in her blankets by the side of the fire, she tossed and turned in a futile bid to give herself needed sleep. Close by, her horse munched grass, glad to be unburdened of saddle and gear after hours of continuous travel. Overhead, the sky was ablaze with stars, glittering points that reminded a body of her smallness in the vastness of infinity, and added mystery old as time to the night.

To Lil, it was not a silent night. Apart from the sigh of an intermittent breeze, she knew what the Indians meant when they said they heard the trees grow, the rocks breathe.

Eventually, with sleep elusive, she got

up and returned to the vantage point where she could look down on Blanche's wagon. Her eyes widened as she saw the rigid conveyance wasn't completely still; it was rocking on its braked wheels. And her ears burned as she heard, carried on the night air, the creak of plank floorboards and moans from human throats.

'I knew that Jezebel would get up to something like this!' she thought. 'Well, I guess it's good to know I'm not the only one losing sleep.' Then she admonished herself for the bitterness of her thoughts. She had no right to them, and the past had proven it a mistake to let Jackson get under her skin.

The wagon wasn't in a good place by Lil's reckoning. It looked too much like sitting in a trap, but Jackson had no doubt settled on it because it was sheltered, offered kindling and dead wood for easy gathering, and had the best waterhole in miles.

Maybe she was letting foolish emotions cloud her judgement; maybe the

116

two lovemakers did have nothing to fear. It was then, as she sought to reassure herself this was so, that she heard the exchange of cries between the coyotes.

Her ear for such matters was finely attuned. Maybe her own wild nature was kindred to the wilderness itself. Whatever the intricacies of it, the cries didn't ring perfectly true. They could be counterfeit.

Coyotes? Or artful Indians simulating the tongue of the beasts to pass messages of their own?

All the previous day her fullest attention had been on outguessing Jackson Farraday and keeping herself hidden. It struck her with sudden clarity how possible it was that she, too, had been outguessed; that the game-playing white people had been shadowed by unseen redmen.

Using skills that would do credit to a guerrilla fighter, she began a careful reconnaissance. She slipped furtively between the deeper darknesses of rock outcropping, tree bole and clump of brush. It was country she knew her way around blindfold, every dip and fold.

By the time the first grey hints of dawn were sneaking across the eastern ridges, she'd ascertained the worst. The vicinity was plumb crawling with Apaches.

'The landscape's lousy with 'em, like a cur-dog with fleas,' she admitted to herself.

It was a soul-chilling discovery. In every other shadowy place, a copper-coloured figure crouched, waiting for the light that would herald attack on the lone, puny, defenceless wagon of the presumptuous white-eyes.

8

WOMAN TROUBLE, INDIAN TROUBLE

Jackson Farraday roused from the sleep of exhaustion, disturbed by a rapping that came from under his head. He immediately thought of the wagon toolbox. Fixed to the left side in back of the lazyboard, it pulled out in front of the rear left wheel and contained hatchets, an auger, a saw, a selection of nails, bolts and pins, plus a coil of spare rope.

They were all items that might attract a common thief in town, but recall of his whereabouts, tucked away in a brush-grown draw among open hills, made the noise a more disconcerting worry. Besides, the sounds had an urgency and regularity that didn't fit with an explanation of petty thieving.

119

Hoarsely spoken words were added to the repeated taps on the underside of the wagon bed. 'Jackson! Jackson Farraday, wake up, you mutt!'

Jackson jerked erect in sheer, incredulous surprise.

'Huh . . . what in hell — ?'

'It's me — Lilian Goodnight,' the voice said. 'Let down the tailgate. We've got to talk.'

'Misfit Lil! Blast you! What right — ?'

'Let me in and I'll tell you!'

It was no place or time to hold a stupid conversation. 'I'm busy,' he growled back. 'Clear out, you pesky brat!'

Lil's voice rasped again, urgent and irritated. 'I've had to circle round, then Injun my way through rocks and brush to get to your rotten wagon. I ain't skedaddling anywhere. Let me in, Jackson.'

Beside him, Blanche rose from her prone position, pushing up on to her elbows, wearing nothing but a gold ring on her finger.

'Who're you talking to, Jackson?' she asked, bleary-eyed and displaying her abundant self indecorously.

'It's Miss Goodnight. I'll have to see what's she's on about.'

Lil's ears caught his words. 'I'm on about 'Paches. We're about surrounded by 'em, Jackson. You gotta back it on up, turn it around, and drive outa here like smoke before the sun's up — it's your only chance!'

Blanche's eyes popped out of her head as she recognized Lil's voice.

'Good God, the waitress slut from Silver Vein! She must be losing her mind, following us out here. We don't need her underfoot.'

But Jackson had moved and was letting the tailgate down on its chains.

'She's known as more than a waitress, Blanche — '

'I don't care what she's known as! Tell her to go away this instant, you big lummox!'

Women were creatures whose nature largely mystified Jackson. His view was that he didn't care for any female temperament. Now he had two of them upset with him. He was a 'mutt' and a 'lummox', they said. But he respected Lil's judgement in wilderness matters. She knew its lore almost as well as himself.

'I can't tell her to go away,' he told Blanche. 'It sure ain't me who asked her along. Nor is it only a case of being known as — there's those as *are*. Young Lil Goodnight is a frontierswoman through and through.'

Like Lil, he knew the Indian avoided fighting at night because if he was killed in action, he believed his soul would wander aimlessly through all eternity. Sunrise was oft-times the signal for an Indian ambush to be sprung.

Blanche realized everything that mattered was still showing and scrabbled to cover herself with a blanket, but with Jackson's help Lil was already hoisting herself into the wagon.

'I don't care what you say she is,' Blanche snarled. 'This is an outrage!'

Jackson decided right then that though Blanche Kilkieran wasn't hard to look at, she wasn't easy to listen to.

'Life has its little ups and downs,' Lil said, as sweetly as she ever said anything. 'Right now, you're getting all upset about a very little one, Mrs Kilkieran. I'm not here to make you eat crow on account of being caught sleeping with another man, but to let you know you're in danger of losing your bleached scalp!'

Blanche's face was dead white, except for small patches of scarlet on her cheekbones, but her eyes were blazing with fury.

'She's loaded on whiskey,' she accused. 'I can smell it on her breath. Throw her back out straight away!'

'Ladies — calm down!' Jackson said.

'Ain't me who's busting her buttons,' Lil said. 'Mrs Kilkieran might be . . . ' cept in point of fact she ain't wearing any to bust! My advice to the both of you lovebirds' — that mockingly — 'is get into your duds pronto.'

Exposed hypocrite that she was, Blanche was shaking. 'Teach the brat to bridle her tongue, Jackson!' she snapped.

'She might be right, Blanche,' Jackson said, reaching for his pants.

Snorting her indignation and trying not to lose her dignity, Blanche also made moves to recover her clothing. 'You mean you believe this farrago about Apaches?'

'Why ever not?' Jackson turned to Lil. 'By what miracle do you think we can get our tails out of this crack, Lil?'

'The Injuns are on all sides 'cept the west, 'cos that way lies the river and they reckon you can't cross it.'

'Well, it is in full and icy flow from the spring melt. Could be they've got it figured aright.'

'Oh, God, we're doomed!' Blanche wailed.

'No, they haven't,' Lil said, ignoring the interruption from the Preacher's adulterous woman. 'They've forgotten Buckmeyer's old ford. It gives you the one chance to get over and away.'

'Buckmeyer . . . by heaven, you're on to something, Lil!'

Jackson was, once again, amazed by Lil's intricate and extensive knowledge of her homeland. Buckmeyer was a freighter, long passed on, who'd sunk many huge, flat stones to the silty and soft riverbed to save him a long, circuitous trip to a now forgotten and abandoned logging camp. The surprising part was that this had all happened before cattleman Goodnight's girl had been born.

'Sure, I'm on to our best hope, Jackson,' Lil said, 'but I'd hate to hang by my toes till *she's* gotten into them frilly drawers. Quit gawking and give me the loan of a rifle, will you? I'll cover you while you hitch the wagon.'

'Someone should have taken a slipper to you years ago,' Blanche grumbled waspishly under her breath.

Lil was quick to retort. 'It was tried, but all they got was hot and lickerish for their trouble.'

'Jackson, shut her up!'

But he'd taken himself off. In the half-light of the ending night, he unhobbled the wagon's horses, a docile pair, and swiftly harnessed them to the wagon pole, carefully leaving the breast straps and traces loose enough to let the pole swing sideways if the front wheels hit an obstacle on a fast run over rough ground. The activity didn't escape notice.

The watching hostiles began the impending, inevitable attack.

'They're a-coming, Jackson!' Lil cried.

He heard the crack of the Henry he'd given Lil. Leaping for the wagon seat, he saw a party of bronzefaced men who'd plainly been creeping up on his camp dash out from the cover of some huge boulders and make for the moving wagon, whooping gleefully and armed with tomahawks and broad-bladed knives. They were Apaches with long, straight black hair encircled by wide headbands.

The shot fired by Lil hadn't been expected and gave them pause — especially when it was seen that the slug had sliced through the large eagle feather stuck in the apparent leader's head-band. The eagle was considered by the Apaches the proudest and most victorious of all birds. Hence the most respected warriors always wore eagles' feathers and claws. The Apache dived to the ground and rolled out of sight.

Those who didn't follow his example quickly discovered they were an easy mark for the markswoman in the wagon, who continued firing in grim earnest at amazing speed. The ambushers had never seen such shooting. Several of the more rash were hit, doubled up, and pitched face down in the dust. One went down with a shrill scream.

The rest scattered into cover, and those who carried them unslung bows.

The wagon lurched out of the draw.

To Jackson's surprise, Lil then said to neither himself or Blanche in particular, 'I'll need my pony.'

Immediately, she took a flying leap from the seat of the wagon and landed on her feet like a cat in the tall grass, still clutching the rifle.

Jackson tugged at the lines and reached for the brake, but the horses, lashed into a run, had the bits between their teeth and were pulling hard.

Lil yelled after him, 'Keep rolling, Jackson!'

Nobody could say Misfit Lil lacked grit, but he felt darkly pessimistic of her chances — alone, on foot, at least temporarily, and up against blood-thirsty renegade Indians.

'Where's she going?' Blanche cried.

'For help,' Jackson said at a guess, though his hopes that she'd get through and back with an army detail in time to make any difference were faint.

At a dizzying, teeth-rattling speed, the wagon was now heading downhill toward the river. Jackson again reached for, and this time clamped on, the brake in an attempt to bring the wagon's flight under control. Sparks flew from the iron-shod wheels.

The panic-stricken horses were barely checked.

Another chilling development was that a larger band of Apaches had emerged from the broken landscape, goading their wiry, fleet-footed mustangs unmercifully into pursuit, and yipping excitedly.

From inside the swaying, jolting wagon, Blanche screamed, 'Stop, Jackson Farraday! You'll kill us!'

Jackson knew stopping was not an option. Though he did his best, he considered it as much luck as judgement that he was able to steer the crazed wagon team along the river-bank to the rotted stump that had once been the stake marking Buckmeyer's Ford.

He wound the lines round his arms and put all his strength into a desperate heave on the right horse that put the wagon into a slither around the old marker.

The left-side wheels lifted off the ground, whirring and hurling dust and particles of rock. For a moment, Jackson's heart lurched into his mouth. He thought the rigid, upright vehicle might actually tip on to its side, but it righted itself with a bone-jarring thump and hurtled on toward the water.

Behind him, several of the chasing Indians had begun using their relics of firearms. Balls of lead whistled past his head.

Maybe stung by one or other of these long, spent shots, the horses didn't slow but plunged into the full river.

Splash and froth flew in blinding curtains around them. Jackson could tell that they'd hit the narrow ford with miraculous accuracy only because they weren't instantly swept away. Even so, the hectic pace of galloping horses and wagon was slowed by the powerful lateral tug of flowing water several feet deep.

Perhaps predictably, over the years of disuse, the stones sunk by Buckmeyer had shifted and moved in the mud of the river bottom. The wagon was only partly across when the rim of the left front wheel crashed into the edge of a big, tip-tilted rock that rose a good six inches above the general level of the causeway.

The result was catastrophic. The iron tyre sprung off and the wheel disintegrated, one spoke cracking and the rest flying loose from the black-gum hub and the splintered rim. The frantic horses kept pulling right up to the moment the critically damaged wagon tipped completely on its side with a splashing crash and they could drag it no further. Then, finding their progress arrested, the pair snorted and pranced wildly.

'Oh God!' Blanche hollered from inside. 'You fool, Jackson! We'll break our necks! We'll be drowned!'

Jackson spoke roughly in an attempt to compose her. 'Stop whining, woman! Climb out of there and get ready to swim. It's maybe the only way we'll make it to the other side.'

'I can't swim,' she revealed, following it with a moan that was a ghastly travesty of those he'd heard her emit under shared blankets. 'I'm staying here!'

'Are you loco? You can't if you want to live out the day untouched.'

He slashed deftly at the wagon's canvas with a well-honed hunting knife and hauled her out on to its unsteady side. She gave him a minimum of co-operation.

'This is unspeakable! I'm paying you to guide and protect me,' she asserted with a defiant crabbiness.

'Stay here and the Apaches'll take you for sure,' he said. 'What they'd do to you would be worse than drowning, I reckon.'

'You mean the savages would rape me?'

'Bluntly, that'd be only the half of it. They'd put you through one helluva time. Some women would prefer a bullet than face an ordeal at these renegades' hands.'

With the damned Apaches milling on the river bank, howling delight, Jackson viewed his grim observations as not a mite previous.

'Dear Jesus! You've delivered me to a

pack of heathen bastards, Farraday!'

'Save your breath, Blanche,' Jackson advised.

Their capture was a prospect he didn't like to think on. Blanche Kilkieran was quite a looker, a woman in her prime. Unprincipled trash that they were, Angry-fist's rebel sub-tribe would take to her bounteous white flesh with a devilish will.

They had to fight.

But Jackson feared whatever he said, or they did, their fates already lay at the torture stake. For the mounted Indians were entering the river, throwing out clouds of spray and uttering jubilant cries.

9

ANGRY-FIST'S CAPTIVES

Misfit Lil had to break through the cordon of hidden Indians to reach her campsite and, she hoped, her waiting pony. Her accurate shooting had thrown a scare into the party that had crept up on the wagon, but she knew the survivors and many other hostiles were still in the offing.

She determined to follow up on her advantage, which was as flimsy as the seven left of the sixteen shots that had been in the magazine tube below the borrowed repeating rifle's barrel.

So far, Jackson's Improved Henry had served her well, scattering the opposition and ridiculing its inferior weaponry. As rapidly as she'd fired, the Henry's barrel had failed to heat or to eject a single cartridge shell, which was a fault she'd noted in other long guns.

Now, much would depend on her own boldness.

If she could win through to Fort Dennis, Colonel Lexborough would be obliged to send out a force, Washington policy be damned! But how long would it all take? Would the assistance be too late?

Suddenly, seven mounted shapes surged out from a shadowy stand of pines. More Apaches! They were masters at disappearing and appearing without warning in this mixed terrain — into nowhere, out of nowhere. They came galloping madly toward her, uttering blood-curdling screeches. They could have shot her down with their short bows, but maybe because they saw she was a woman and wanted to take her uninjured, they hesitated.

It was the instant undoing of two of them. Lil levered and fired. *Crack! Crack!* What for another shooter might have been vain chance was for Lil a certitude. The two leading Apaches pitched dead, or close to it, from their mustangs.

The third rider hauled up so abruptly that his beast reared on its hind legs.

'The girl has magic firestick!' he shrieked to his companions in consternation.

His moment of disbelief gave Lil just the opportunity she needed. The two riderless mustangs had trotted on toward her in aimless puzzlement and, being the half-broken animals the rebel Apaches usually rode, were fit to bolt. Lil grabbed the nearest by a short rein and leaped astride before it could get away.

She clamped her strong legs to its lean flanks and kicked with her heels. It was not a mount a horsewoman would have chosen for the flight she had to make, but maybe she could use it to carry her to her own pony which was of an altogether better breed.

Arrows zipped past her head as the irate Apaches gave chase, now lusting only for her scalp.

Gleefully, the Apaches who'd followed Jackson Farraday and Blanche Kilkieran to the river encircled the capsized wagon and the two palefaces clinging to its battered body.

Their ribald laughter and excited yells told Jackson they fully appreciated one of the certain captives was a woman. He caught rude allusions to rigours the more civilized of Indians would now consider barbaric. Her use by the braves was anticipated with pleasure — an occasion which would be attended by primitive and cruel ceremonies.

Too, he knew enough of their tongue to gather he'd been recognized as the longhaired one who'd chopped their leader Angry-fist's left hand from his arm in a tomahawk duel.

These whites were prizes indeed!

Jackson reached for his holstered revolver. His fingers were closing on the worn butt of it when, from close quarters, came a hurled tomahawk. Some sixth sense gave him warning and he whirled in time to glimpse its cold flash but not to avoid it catching him full on the right temple.

The throw was clever, or very lucky, because it was the flat of the razor-sharp blade that hit him rather than the fatal edge. Stunned by the slamming blow, he toppled from the wagon into the river. He knew vaguely, in his dazed state, that he should feel the ice-cold water, but all sensation had ceased, and his last awareness was of a scream of terror ripped from Blanche's throat. Then it, too, was submerged in a tide of roaring black that became nothingness.

He was out of his head for what must have been several minutes. When consciousness returned, it was to awareness of a jolting pain in his wrists and ankles, which had been tied tightly with grass ropes. His recovery from the river was recent — his clothes still dripped — and he was suspended from a long and sturdy lance threaded through his looped limbs. The lance was carried over the shoulders of four sinewy, jogging warriors, two at each end.

The half-dozen Apaches moving alongside him over a rock-littered flat were in high humour, full of the good reasons to congratulate themselves. They'd captured their chief's sworn enemy alive, plus as a bonus they had another white-eye who was 'plenty woman'.

They could have already slain them and taken their scalps, but that idea did not commend itself. Important prizes like these must be the centre of a torture-feast in their encampment. A full attendance of the community, squaws included, would witness and participate in the many exquisite deeds which would carry the pair to their deaths.

Jackson heard Blanche's frantic voice. 'Get your lewd hands off me, you swine!' Loud guffaws followed her remonstration. Painfully, he twisted his throbbing head.

Blanche's wrists, too, were lashed together tightly but she was on foot, stumbling as they pushed her along like a rag doll. What was left to her of her expensive clothes was torn and she'd been drenched like himself, so the ruins of fine fabrics clung revealingly to her full figure. With rough hands, she was passed from brave to brave. Each enjoyed his chance to touch and feel and poke freely.

'Blanche!' Jackson cried, struggling against the cutting ropes to keep her in sight. 'Are you . . . are you all right?'

'Of course I'm not all right, you fool,' she croaked. 'You can see what this pack are working themselves up to, can't you?'

'I follow their lingo. Nothing much'll happen to you just yet,' Jackson said. It was the best comfort he had to offer.

The sun was a blinding white ball moving toward its zenith in a brassy sky when the prisoners were carried and prodded into Angry-fist's encampment in a high and hidden valley.

In his long career as a trail scout, Jackson had tarried many a winter moon in Indian villages, sharing and learning about the lives of 'red brothers', but none had ever struck him as having quite the coldness and hostility of Angry-fist's rebel camp. No high-pitched laughter from playing children reached his ears. The few squaws present pointed and cackled maliciously — one spat full in his face, the putrid glob trickling to rest in his beard. Two mangy dogs growled and raised their hackles, neck fur bristling.

Well, it was the beginning of what he had to expect. In ending his last enforced sojourn in this rebel band's lodges, he had grievously wounded their hotheaded young chief and set fire to their grass.

'Where are they taking us?' Blanche asked.

'Oh, for now I guess they'll dump us in some smelly wigwam while they stoke up their fires, beat the drums and make ready for a big shindig come dusk.'

Jackson was wrong. They were incarcerated in a stockade made of hardwood saplings, stripped of their bark, driven close together into the ground and roofed with the tattiest of hides.

Blanche, sprawled in the corner where they'd thrown her, protested bitterly.

'Washington should allow the army to exterminate all Indians from our states and territories forthwith. They're vermin!'

Jackson wasn't ready to agree and thought it best she should moderate her criticism.

'I reckon the tribes are the same as white folks — some good, some bad, some in between. Granted, this bunch is all bad. Worse, they figure I've done them wrong. You must deny all friendship with me and act humble if you're to save your scalp.'

But Blanche continued to complain:

she'd been abused grossly, she was thirsty, she was hungry; she'd been misled about Jackson's proficiency by his 'cronies' at Fort Dennis and in Silver Vein . . .

Jackson found it almost a relief when two squaws with greasy hair and a rich reek of gamey body odour came and dragged her away from the bare prison, where to and for what he could only guess.

'The woman has no alliance with me,' Jackson cried, in the dialect he knew them to use. 'She's innocent!'

The two hags sniggered. 'That we shall see, Longhair,' one said.

Finally, when narrow bands of fireglow cut across the stamped dirt floor through the gaps between the saplings, drums began to sound. He heard chanting and the rhythmic slap of moccasined feet, dancing. Then the Apaches came for him.

They hauled him toward the biggest tepee in the camp. By the painting on its stretched skin, clearly visible in the light of a huge celebratory fire, Jackson knew it to be the lodge of his deadly enemy, Angry-fist.

The young chieftain sat imperiously on a crude throne which was no more than a deadfall covered by a thick blanket of rich colours faded by age and dirt. What the charismatic rebel had lost in cockiness and youthful exuberance since Jackson had last seen him, had been replaced with hardness and bitterness.

Under an impressive ceremonial bonnet decorated with ermine tails and eagle feathers, the fire-light revealed a face of new, bleaker planes and deeper lines. His eyes glittered with the intensity of his hatred, but most noticeable of all was the stump of his left wrist, dressed incongruously in a pure white bandage such as only a white person would apply.

Jackson had too much else to take in to wonder . . .

At Angry-fist's feet, Blanche Kilkieran lay trussed in ropes and a blanket — and gagged. Maybe the Apache squaws, too, had tired of her sharp, uncurbed tongue.

The drumming ceased.

'So you are back in my power at last, white dog!' Angry-fist pronounced in a harsh voice that trembled with the relishing of the glorious moment. 'What a fool you are, daring to come within revenge's grasp — you and your soft woman here!'

He stabbed at her with a feathered lance.

Thinking to save Blanche from a share in the punishment that awaited him, Jackson said, 'She ain't my woman, Angry-fist.'

'You lie, Longhair!' Angry-fist rapped. 'I am not stupid. Squaws search this woman, have clever ways to look in right places. Sign tells she was served by a man at last shining of the moon. My braves swear it was not one of them, though each now eagerly awaits his turn, for squaws say she is woman in fullest bloom accustomed to the ways of the flesh, and they have earned their pleasure well.'

Jackson was unable to contain his anger. 'Red trash!' he said in tones of condemnation. 'You can't get away with it. The soldiers — '

Angry-fist leaped up in a rage, setting a necklace of bears' claws rattling. He strode at Jackson — and smashed his right fist into his face. Jackson tasted blood as his lips and mouth were cut by his own teeth.

'This time, all will be as I say, Longhair!' the maimed chieftain roared. 'You shall not cheat the torture stake again, and your woman shall be *our* harlot, till you both die.'

' . . . *Which must not be before the white man's almighty God has received due tribute, Angry-fist!*'

The white-man's voice that boomed from the gloom outside the firelight worked the astonishing trick of defusing Angry-fist's temper before he could strike another blow. The expression of sudden uncertainty on his face — the hovering of his one clenched fist — told the story. He glanced, too, to his bandaged stump apprehensively.

The speaker had a hold over him and was using it as leverage.

Yet more astonishing was the identity of the unseen intervener. The man who stepped forward to show himself — confidently, like a sleek and proud animal asserting his authority over his group — was Patrick Kilkieran.

He laughed at Jackson, who was, and must have looked, dumbfounded.

'Sure it is you recognize me, Mr Farraday. I'm the gent given up for dead, I understand. So touching my dear wife should have brought you looking for me . . . '

The cat-yellow eyes under the heavy lids held a smouldering glint as he appreciated her unlovely, silenced predicament. 'Isn't it, Blanche?'

10

KILKIERAN'S PLOT

When Misfit Lil commandeered the loose Apache mustang, her thoughts ran in turmoil. Both speed and reliability were called for, which was but one reason why she returned to her campsite and switched mounts to her familiar grey cow pony, Rebel, a superb animal she'd trained herself from a foal.

Keenly aware the swift little mustangs of her surviving enemies were gaining on her, she turned when coming close to the place she'd left her horse and gear and rapidly fired her remaining shots. The rifle weighed a sight more than seven pounds but could be held in one hand and fired as a revolver.

Deadshot that she was, however, it was mighty difficult to hit moving targets from the back of a speeding, half-wild mustang. Only with the fifth and last shot did she strike lucky.

'Got yuh!' she said in satisfaction, as the leading bronze rider threw up his arms and tumbled headlong.

The following mustang immediately careened into the checked, riderless beast. Both hit the dust in a rolling mess of threshing legs and squeals.

Bodies were crushed. A skull cracked on impact with a rock and a neck was broken.

It was enough to give the pursuing party reason to pause. Howls of dismay rent the air. Lil used the moments before they could reform to throw saddle and bedroll on to Rebel in double-quick time.

Before she finished, some of the red warriors had managed to fit arrows to bowstrings. They let fly a shower of wicked shafts which pattered disconcertingly around her.

Not wanting the Henry to fall into renegade hands, her final task was to swing the emptied rifle against a rock, snapping the barrel from the walnut stock. She had no further use for its encumbrance. From now on, she'd have to rely on only her two loaded six-shooters.

She was up and streaking away when the main body of her pursuers brought their wiry mustangs under control. Seeing she was on horse again, a signal was given to resume the deadly chase.

Their fury redoubled, the party let out terrifying war cries and thundered after her.

Lil headed the fresh grey pony back toward the river, but further upstream, hoping to draw at least some Apaches away from the ford and Jackson and Blanche. Maybe in more mountainous, rugged terrain she could capitalize on her horsewoman's skills and her superior pony to shake off pursuit and make it all the way to Fort Dennis and help.

But she knew that she'd have to ride like the wind and her chances of escape were far from good.

'What have you been playing at here, Patrick Kilkieran?'

'Yeah, what the hell is going on?'

Jackson Farraday put a power of glowering annoyance into his reiteration of Blanche Kilkieran's sharp question.

They'd just been escorted by an aggrieved bunch of young painted braves, about naked except for breech-clouts, to a cabin on the very edge of Angry-fist's makeshift village. In the poor light, Jackson had made out a drift of woodsmoke from a tin chimney, lamplight through crudely chinked logs and the torn hessian curtains over the apertures that served as windows. The place was a long-gone mountain man's abandoned abode.

'I'm about to play host, my friend,' Kilkieran said. 'You're handed over to be guests in my humble home.'

A fling of his hand took in the single room, partitioned by a hanging blanket. The unscreened area was furnished with a rough table and chairs, a potbelly stove, and an animal smell. Bear?

'However, Angry-fist's cheated warriors will be keeping close guard to see you don't — uh — reject my hospitality.'

'That doesn't get to the bottom of it,' Jackson remarked, not liking Kilkieran's jeering tone, or his evasion.

The ex-priest remained quietly amused. 'You and my — I understand, erring spouse should be more gracious, Mr Farraday. For the time being, I've saved your pathetic life from slow forfeiture at the torture stake. Blanche I've saved from a fate probably worse than, oh, about three-dozen deaths by my last count of Angry-fist's strength in virile bucks.'

'Cut the smart baloney, Preacher Kilkieran!' Jackson growled. 'How come we're let off?'

'Don't take that tone with me, mister. Were it not highly possible your arrival will do me a big favour, you could both go straight to hell for all I care.'

Blanche's face flamed with anger and embarrassment. 'I'm your *wife*, Kilkieran!'

'Yeah, that's as maybe in a legal sense, but why do you think I really lit out from Colorado? Because I got sick of your never-ending wants and manipulative ways, that's why; tired of the soft life you love so much, of tricking the sick and wealthy elderly out of their money. Moreover, you made no real secret of it you saw yourself as too much woman for one man, Blanche. Well, you ain't! Ask Mr Farraday here whether he's not had better.'

Kilkieran's explanation put Blanche beside herself with fury.

'How dare you ... Jackson, the bastard is insulting us!'

Jackson shuffled uncomfortably. 'Hey! None of this is my fight, but I didn't like what I saw of you in Silver Vein, Kilkieran, and a coyote never changes his bark.'

'Nor a bitch her yap,' Kilkieran said. 'Blanche should've told you outright why she really wanted to find me. It sure ain't because our marriage was made in heaven. It's because Pure Waters Colony is nothing without my reputation and presence as a miracle man — a healer.'

'But that's all hokum and you know it!' Blanche burst out.

Kilkieran shrugged. 'Be it as maybe, soon as I pulled out I bet you had a failing venture on your hands. You had to get me back, so the colony could carry on bringing in the money you needed to lead the grand life. Be honest, Blanche, I bore you. You crave excitement of the salon kind and you've philandered with a procession of men behind my back. They include, I now hear from Angry-fist's people, the doughty Mr Farraday whose alleged skills have gotten you into this mess.'

Jackson kept his temper in check and his released hands in his pockets. Kilkieran's contempt and Blanche's angry humiliation were taking the confrontation down paths marginally relevant.

'He maligns me, Jackson!' Blanche said. She put a dramatic hand somewhere in the region of her probably palpitating heart. 'I swear I'm not a loose woman.'

Jackson ignored her. 'What's your standing with Angry-fist, Kilkieran? Why ain't I dead and Blanche ravished? And what's the favour we've done by coming here?'

Kilkieran sighed, as though exasperated he should be expected to explain.

'You might call me Angry-fist's medicine man. I arranged to come here from Silver Vein to grow him a new hand in place of the one you amputated, Farraday.'

'You *what* . . . ?' Blanche screeched.

'Kinda rich, ain't it? Even for me. These Indians are simple souls, believing in magic and superstition, all kinds of rot. Their faith in the Great Spirit, or whatever name they call Him by, makes

Christians' faith look narrow and niggardly. Didn't figure me for an Indian-lover, did you, Blanche?'

'Why would you promise Angry-fist such a thing, Kilkieran?' Jackson wanted to know.

'You might as well hear — not as though it'll do you any good. The gang that cleaned out the Ranchers' and Miners' Bank in Silver Vein was led by a man I recognized from an earlier part of my life as Yuma Nat Hawkins.'

'That scoundrel,' Jackson murmured. 'You'd be vultures both, if of a different feather.' He remembered Lilian Goodnight's almost instant and seemingly instinctive animosity for the man who'd eventually abused her friend Estelle. Her suspicion . . .

Kilkieran, sure he had the whiphand, disregarded Jackson's insult.

'Yuma Nat has a hideout in these mountains, I learned — his own robbers' roost, his own Hole-in-the-Wall. I figured Angry-fist is the only one with the knowledge and the manpower to

156

take the place, which is reputedly heavily fortified and guarded. In exchange for using my magic powers to give him a hand, the deal was he'd wipe out Yuma Nat and I'd secure all of the gang's loot that was worthless to the redman, including the haul from Silver Vein and other robberies.'

Jackson nodded his head as he began to get the picture. 'And I take it Angry-fist hasn't delivered yet because you haven't delivered.'

'Aw, I was working around to persuading him anyway, and your turning up was just what it took to clinch it. I've told him it was the power of my mind over Blanche's that enabled me to use her to lure his worst enemy into a situation where his war-party could capture him . . . Cunning, huh?'

'But it's all lies!' Blanche protested.

'Sure, but it looks like it's gonna work fine and dandy. Farraday's delivery into Angry-fist's hands — should I say hand? — is seen by him as a good omen.'

Jackson's contempt for Kilkieran grew. So did the chill the man brought to his spine. 'Something encouraged by yourself, I guess.'

'Of course. I've told him it's proof the white man's Almighty God is on his side, but that He now calls for Yuma Nat's loot as suitable tribute before he can be permitted to indulge in the pleasure of torturing you lovebirds to death.' Kilkieran chuckled. 'Why, I do allow Angry-fist hates you so bad, Farraday, he'd accept your grisly death as exchange enough for wiping out Yuma Nat, and to hell with the new hand!'

Jackson said, 'I hope when the Apaches get wise to your false tongue they hack it out before they scalp you. I'm surprised they've haven't done it already.'

Impenitent, Kilkieran sniggered. 'Ah, Farraday, you don't know what good terms I'm on with these Apaches.' He faced his wife. 'There's something I must tell you, Blanche.'

'Tell it then!'

'They not only let me keep my hair on, they've given me one of their youngest and prettiest women to be my squaw.'

'You've taken a woman?' Blanche was aghast. 'A filthy Indian whore?'

'Sure, Blanche. Didn't I say? I'm an *Indian* lover now!'

'You bastard, Kilkieran! A squawman . . . you disgust me.'

'Relax, Blanche — she ain't in no wise filthy, and I've taught her how to make a stew like a good American wife, Apache food being apt to be burnt or blood-raw. Coffee, too. I'll get her to serve us some of both presently, so's you can make yourselves at home.'

He clapped his hands and a slim shape with bare bronze limbs emerged shyly from behind the hanging blanket.

'I thought I could smell something rank in here!' Blanche said.

'I call her Little Dove,' Kilkieran said, unperturbed by his wife's verdict.

The Indian girl was about young

enough to be the Preacher's daughter, Jackson thought, and Kilkieran had been right to call her pretty.

She was no stocky, slab-faced creature of doubtful breeding, but a young beauty with raven-black, shiny hair. She was of medium height and slim build, but too strong-looking to be considered a waif. Small breasts thrust with unwitting pride at a raggedly hemmed, scanty dress of soft-beaten hide. Doe-like brown eyes fixed on Kilkieran attentively, dutifully. Jackson guessed she was indeed the best the sub-tribe had to offer.

'Say howdy, folks,' Kilkieran said. 'The gal's gotten some other, impossible Apache name I can't get my tongue around, but she'll answer to Little Dove.'

Jackson wasn't about to visit his anger on the young woman. She was probably a heap more sinned against than sinning. He nodded amiably. 'Howdy, Little Dove.'

The girl dipped her head, but when her eyes travelled to Blanche they took on a jealous, possessive gleam she didn't have the art to conceal.

'She old squaw of One-Who-Cures?' she asked.

'Very old squaw,' Kilkieran agreed maliciously.

'It is good that she is old,' Little Dove responded.

To the others, Kilkieran said as an aside, 'You see, the Apache woman not only subscribes to compliance and effacement, she speaks the truth at all times. Only white women speak with crooked tongues!'

Lost for words, the insulted Blanche spat like an incensed cat. 'She stinks, Kilkieran!'

'You can't get everything in trade for a coupla jars of redeye, Blanche, and I tell you, the fragrance don't matter a damn when it comes down to satisfying a male appetite for new and younger flesh. Besides, not to put too fine a point on it, your own paramour, Mr Farraday, don't exactly smell like roses either.'

'She isn't decently dressed!' Blanche accused.

Little Dove wasn't ignorant. She struck a cold, haughty pose. 'Old white woman not like me.'

Her finding, being obvious to everyone, was ignored.

'Oh, I kinda like the natural-woman look,' Kilkieran mused, as if politely reflecting on Blanche's observation. 'Though you could be right. She'd look considerable sweeter in pretty boots and stockings than with naked feet and legs. What did Angry-fist's squaws do with yours, eh, Blanche?'

Jackson looked Kilkieran straight in the eye.

'Preacher, I've got a hunch the way you treat women will get you killed some day.'

11

LIL'S LEAP

The Apaches' fleet-footed mustangs, unhampered by the weight and refinements of saddle trappings, were gaining ground on Misfit Lil's grey pony with every stride. She turned in the saddle and loosed revolver shots to deter them.

It was after such a moment of inattention to the direction taken by her straining pony that she turned to find herself on a wrong trail.

'Shit, we're heading for a dead end!' she gasped. She remembered the trail as one that led to a bluff towering sixty feet over the river where it carved its bed through increasingly mountainous country.

What was she to do?

Her pursuers had been whittled down in immediate number to a mere two, both of them better warriors than their erstwhile comrades in every respect. They were better riders and their prowess at some stage had also understandably rewarded them with the best of such rifles as Angry-fist's bunch possessed.

Lil decided a turnabout was nigh impossible faced with such enemies. She had no option but to urge Rebel on. She crouched low in the saddle, leaned along her pony's neck and patted it encouragingly. A slug whistled over her head.

It was the last. The two Apaches vented yells of victory. They thought they had her trapped; that her scalp and any other parts were good as theirs.

Lil had held in her hands once the obscene horror of an Indian pouch fashioned from the cured breast skin of a mutilated woman. 'Ain't that somethin'?' the trophy's vile owner had crowed. The sickening memory was enough to spur her on.

'It's risky, but the hell with it! Those

sadistic scum ain't hacking bits off me for fancy knick-knacks . . . '

Behind her the two excited Apaches were streaking in for the kill — grinning, now no longer wasting shells on her. They knew well enough that straight ahead lay a cliff with a sheer drop to the boiling spring floodstream of the river, hissing its way through the ravine at the bluff's foot and on down the mountainside to rapids some two miles lower.

Lil galloped on pell-mell, not letting them close the gap another yard and as though a country mile of clear trail stretched ahead.

'We've got to risk it, pardner,' she told Rebel and herself. 'I know you're a fearless jumper and a good swimmer, but this'll be the real test.'

Calculating her chances coolly, she tightened her knees on the gallant grey and shortened her hold on the reins. Without hesitation, the pony boldly launched into empty space.

Then Lil was out in the air, like an

arrow from a bow, with nothing below but an expanse of swift-flowing water, dark with shadow.

The long seconds of the fall were a new and exhilarating experience she knew she'd never forget. It culminated in shock that momentarily blacked her out.

The water roared in her ears. Fed by snows melting upstream, it felt icy and endlessly deep.

It said much for her instinctive skills as a horsewoman that she didn't part company with the saddle during the plunge. When woman and horse bobbed to the surface of the river, the huge, high splash of displaced water was still crashing back down behind them.

They were caught up, spun around twice and swept rapidly downstream by the strong current.

Meanwhile, the Apache pursuit came to a slithering halt on the rim above. The mustangs the pair rode did not share the grey's unbalking confidence in his rider. Half-tamed animals, they reared in panic before the drop. Though tough and wiry, they were not proficient jumpers. Sight of the roaring water set them off along the skyline upstream. The warriors on their backs fought to pull them up and regain mastery.

Lil lost sight of them. The invisible force of the rushing river swept the grey along helplessly. All struggle was useless, though the game animal tried to flounder toward the opposite bank. Lil's realization of this served to sharpen her anguish at the predicament she'd thrown them into.

'Still, if this kills us we'll have a clean death,' she rasped, 'which is more'n the 'Paches would've given us.'

Moreover, she was still in the saddle, able to give what encouragement she could to her pony and to pull up his head a little, out of the full, disturbing thrust of the water. Lil, if not the horse, had a good understanding of the premise that it was futile to expend energy on circumstances you were powerless to change.

Sometimes, she thought ironically, a girl was obliged to go with the flow, conserving strength until the situation altered.

And so it panned out. The swift, swirling current spun them continually until Lil found herself getting dizzy. Then, at the end of a particularly mad whirl, they were amazingly in quieter water, spluttering and gasping for breath.

The grey found himself suddenly, surprisingly, treading water in a calm hole. He responded by swimming back to the bank and was about to clamber out of the water when Lil caught the familiar sound of pounding, unshod hoofs.

'Goddamnit . . . ' she murmured. It could only be her Apache pursuers, checking the river for evidence of a dead horse and a dead girl.

She was in a tricky corner. Had her daring leap and the river only delivered her back into the renegades' hands?

She slipped quickly out of the saddle

into the water. Swimming strongly herself, she pulled Rebel after her upstream to where a large outcropping of red sandstone overhung the stream, its base partially eroded from under it by the incessant action of the lapping river. The trail along the river-bank passed over the ledge of rock in such a way that the deep hollow beneath would be effectively hidden from the view of anyone above.

The hoofbeats came to a halt above her and Lil heard two voices speaking in the Apache lingo. Clapping a hand hard over her pony's nostrils, she held her breath and listened.

The two Apaches dismounted. From their mutterings she gathered they stood on the rock immediately above her, scanning the rushing water.

'The white woman has vanished. Did you see her swept under, brother?'

'She went very fast,' the other replied, but plainly in doubt of Lil's fate.

The first brave didn't want to risk his

neck, exploring at closer quarters the dangerous, icy water. One white woman's scalp could be worth only so much.

'There are no tracks along the bank to prove she has come out of the river,' he said.

The second brave decided to take a pragmatic line.

'True,' he grunted. 'But nor are there bodies. Maybe they have been flushed on and over the rapids. I suggest we rejoin our brothers but speak only indirectly of the white's whereabaouts. They would heap scorn on us for not slaying her, since we carry the best firesticks which kill at great distances. If we had seen this daring woman again, we could have shot her to be sure. But we will have to say the river took her instead.'

Lil heard the Indians return to their horses and leave the high vantage point, still unaware that she'd been right under their noses.

'Well done, Rebel,' she said, releasing

and rubbing the pony's nose. 'Gee, that was a close call and no mistake!'

She led him upstream along the river's edge. Once or twice they floundered on the treacherous bottom, and they were hindered in places by the rapid current. But Lil fought on doggedly, avoiding being pulled out again into the midstream flow.

'A second battle with the might of the river would be fatal for certain sure,' she told herself grimly.

Presently, she came to shallows and a sandspit from which they were able to wade ashore. The pony shook himself, snorted once or twice. Lil figured thankfully that he had the bred-in bottom left to continue the ride.

Lil was sodden and battered. The flush of jubilation over the hoodwinking of the Apaches was warming, but she had shivery regrets over the delay the chase had occasioned. And she'd lost her whiskey bottle in the river. The swallow left in it would have been a welcome gulp.

'Time to get away from here, Rebel,' she told the grey, urging him into a run.

Jackson Farraday and Blanche Kilkieran had no one to rely on outside of herself to bring them relief from the Apaches. She'd no idea whether they'd successfully crossed the river at Buckmeyer's Ford and escaped Angry-fist's ambush party — she realized they could have been seized — but whatever had happened they were going to need the intervention of the United States Army to regain safety.

That was if they hadn't already met a violent end and remained alive and free once she'd ridden flat-out to Fort Dennis and returned with a troop of cavalry . . .

★　★　★

In the cabin that stank like a bear's den, Patrick Kilkieran slurped coffee brewed and served by his submissive squaw, Little Dove. It was the next morning after he'd temporarily saved Jackson and Blanche from the torture stake.

He smacked his lips and belched to indicate to the young Apache woman in appropriate manner that the coffee was acceptable.

Jackson sipped his own coffee — it was good — but Blanche shuddered in distaste at her estranged husband's behaviour.

'Angry-fist is agreeable,' Kilkieran told his unwilling guests. 'We're going to ride out and raid Yuma Nat's hideout tomorrow at dawn. By sundown I'll have a fortune and your reprieve'll be over. So sorry 'bout that, gentle-folk . . . '

He was in a high old humour and pinched Little Dove's passing bottom, making her squeal — whether in pain or appreciation it was hard to tell.

Blanche curled her lip. 'Stinking heathen slut! How in hell a decent white man could sink so low to touch a lousy squaw, let alone live with and bed one, I'll never grasp.'

'White woman crazy-jealous,' Little

Dove hissed back. 'She no good for any man — should watch Little Dove for lesson.' Hands on hips, she leaned backwards from her knees to buck her slim loins toward Blanche indelicately and rotate them. She finished the performance with an upward thrust of her index finger and a giggling laugh at Blanche's furious red face.

'My God, Kilkieran, she's utterly corrupt!' Blanche cried. 'You've got a lot to answer for!'

'Calm down, ladies!' Kilkieran said. 'Once tomorrow's done and Yuma Nat's loot is mine, you'll have call to tolerate each other's company no longer.'

Jackson coughed. 'If you don't mind my saying so, I wouldn't count your chickens, Kilkieran. You ever see that robbers' roost? Yuma Nat might just hold off a bunch of savage Indians.'

'No, I've not seen Hawkins's place.' He shrugged. 'Won't make a jot of diff'rence, I reckon. The gang'll turn yellow belly up when we ride in. Who'd dare face a scrap ag'inst three score 'Pache warriors with their danders up?'

Jackson assured him evenly, 'Yuma Nat might. He's no back-country chucklehead. Had he turned his inventive mind and organizing skills in other directions, there's no telling what he might have become — banker, railroad baron, statesman. Maybe he just had an unfortunate childhood and took a wrong turn someplace. I wouldn't know. But he's gotten his headquarters fixed like a fortress.'

'Sure,' Kilkieran assented. 'He always was a cunning bastard when I knew him. Do tell about his hideaway, Mr Farraday. You know this country well, I understand, and I'd be most obliged.'

'I owe you no favours, Kilkieran, but I count it a pleasure to let you know what you're going up against.'

Jackson gathered his recollections.

'It's in bleak and barren country. Sand. Rocks. Sage and sparse bunch-grass. The main house sits among scattered cedars back of a five-mile circular flat with lookout points on all sides. Set angled to it are barns, bunkhouses, and a mess or saloon. Pasture and corrals for rustled stock. Beyond the cedar groves rises a ragged wall of pink rock, riddled with caves. The outlaws use 'em to store loot and weapons and food. What does Angryfist know about siege warfare?'

Kilkieran snorted scornfully. 'The Apache are warriors in their own right, mister. Reservation life aside, they're bred to it. Your lack of faith is surprising.'

'Don't preach to me, Preacher! I've said my piece. You'll be a damned fool to rely on a bunch of murderous and thieving Injun renegades in the battle you're proposing. You really think they can pull the thing off?'

Patrick Kilkieran's hard, bright eyes regarded Jackson unwaveringly. He smiled.

'Hell, yes, Farraday. They're that anxious to get their skinning knives working on you and the voluptuous Blanche!'

12

TERSE PARLEY AT FORT DENNIS

Misfit Lil could feel her heart pounding within the cage of her ribs. The hardy grey pony, though hard as nails, was about all in and breathing roughly. Even so, they approached the open gates of Fort Dennis at a commendable lope. After the day's ordeals, Lil reckoned it a miracle the trusty animal could furnish so steady a gait.

She shut her ears to the shouts of protest from the men on guard duty.

'Stop, missy, an' state your business!'

'Faith, it's that pesky colleen Misfit Lil! The saints pertect us from the sergeant's wrath!'

She rode past and in. The truth was Lil didn't figure on the garrison's list of favoured guests — hadn't since she'd flooded its privies in a bizarre and ultimately successful furthering of her bid with Jackson Farraday to foil a gun-running plot.

Time was too precious to waste at this last stage of her desperate ride. She cut Rebel full-tilt across some newly sown grass, paying no respect to a 'keep off' sign.

She reined in before the stone-built administration block's front porch. The winded pony staggered. Foam dripped from flaring nostrils and Lil thought she could see steam curling off his lathered flanks.

Rebel was the strongest, fastest and surest-footed mount she'd ever known. She hoped she hadn't ridden the tough and spirited friend into the ground — his death for Jackson Farraday's and Blanche Kilkieran's lives. She paused to pat his head reassuringly.

'Easy, boy, easy! Don't go to your knees now. We've made it!'

She dropped the reins, swung down, aching in every limb, and ran up the building's steps, boots clopping clumsily on the smooth stone.

Haste — the urgent desire to enlist real assistance for Jackson and the fool Kilkieran woman before it was too late — finally became her undoing. She was less than cautious as she turned into the bare, echoing corridor that contained the office of the commandant, Colonel Brook Lexborough.

In response to her hurried, ringing footfalls, a door swung open behind her after she passed.

'That's far enough, Miss Goodnight!'

The taut command came like the thunderclap that heralds an expected storm. Lil was startled though she knew she shouldn't have been. She stopped dead in mid-stride. Not because she recognized the voice or chose to comply with the implied request, but because it was accompanied by the ominous click of a thumbed-back hammer.

She turned on her accoster. 'Mike Covington! What the hell do you mean, pointing a revolver at me?'

The impeccably accoutred, officious young lieutenant was the last person she wanted to see at this juncture, least of all grimly fisting his shiny, Army model Colt six-shooter so it menaced her fluttering midriff at close range.

'You've got a gall, young woman!' he answered. 'What do *you* mean, busting in here like a bat out of Hades? If it's the colonel you were planning on bothering, it's after hours and his appointment book is filled for two weeks. So you'd best forget it, turn around and get on out!'

Practically wild with frustration, chest tight, Lil said, 'Don't you ever learn, you big sap? Stop acting like a damn fool. You insult me. Would I be wanting to see Lexborough thisaway if it weren't a matter of life or death?'

Covington hesitated, uncertainty showing on his clean-cut, even-featured face. He had a playhouse actor's good looks, but his quandary was surely no act. It was all the chance Lil needed.

Suddenly, swift as a striking wildcat, she lashed at his wavering gun arm with a booted foot.

The gun was sent flying from his grip to hurtle against the wall, causing the cocked hammer to fall on the loaded chamber. The passage filled with the roar and smell of exploding powder. Eardrums were momentarily deadened and noses wrinkled at the acridity.

Colonel Brook Lexborough's door was thrown open.

'What's going on out here?' rumbled the fort's much-harassed commanding officer. He was a tall man in his late fifties, heavily built, with crinkled, iron-grey hair and piercing eyes that missed little.

Covington's face flushed to an embarrassed red.

'Mike — er — Lieutenant Michael Covington was showing me his gun and it kinda went off, Colonel,' Lil said.

The colonel's look was disbelieving. 'Lieutenants in the United States Army don't clown with firearms, young lady,' he growled.

There was a short, awkward silence as Covington and Misfit Lil exchanged accusatory looks. Then the perspicacious colonel said, 'You look a sight tuckered, gal. What's this about? What's brought you here in such a state?'

Lil seized the invitation. She spilled her whole trouble-fraught story. When she was done, Lexborough sighed gustily.

'I shouldn't commit the army to action against the Apache without approval from Washington, and you know it, Miss Goodnight. Mr Farraday is a competent man who should have known better. Mrs Kilkieran was set on a futile search from the outset. Why, her husband has probably been dead a full five months — '

'But Angry-fist's gone on the warpath, I swear!' Lil blurted. 'You have to send a rescue party for Mr Farraday and Mrs Kilkieran before the renegades kill them!'

'Could be they're lost already, too, like Preacher Kilkieran.'

'The army has to try,' Lil implored, her eyes bright and glistening with unshed tears. 'Jackson — Mr Farraday might be holding 'em off single-handed . . . exhausted, refusing to give in . . . '

Her anguished plea melted the colonel's older heart.

'Very well,' he conceded gruffly. 'It's too late in the day to act now, of course . . . Lieutenant Covington, at first light, you'll go with C Troop to check out Miss Goodnight's report.'

'It's the truth, Colonel Lexborough! Can't we go now?'

'Oh, are you going, too?' Lexborough said, gentle mockery in his deep voice. 'As for an earlier departure, it will be too dark to make worthwhile progress. We're in for a moonless night and I'm sorry, I'm in no position to assign men or mounts to what would be dangerous folly.'

Next morning, when Lil at last left the garrison with Michael Covington and C Troop, she was acutely conscious that a full day had elapsed since she'd bailed out of Blanche and Farraday's wagon, leaving them to their own devices and the dubious mercies of the Apache rebels.

★ ★ ★

Not much later than Misfit Lil was leaving Fort Dennis with the long line of blue-clad soldiers, Patrick Kilkieran was leaving the rebel sub-tribe's camp with Angry-fist and his raiding party. They aimed to be placed strategically around Yuma Nat Hawkins's hideout long before the day was out, ready for a swift and devastating attack at sunrise on the morrow.

Jackson Farraday and Blanche Kilkieran were left bound hand and foot in Kilkieran's cabin, watched over by Little Dove and assured by Kilkieran that enough other Apaches would be staying close at hand to assist her if they tried to escape.

As the day wore on, Jackson became uncomfortably aware that the young Indian woman was surreptitiously weighing up his masculinity with darting looks of her sensuous eyes. Any childlike quality she may have possessed derived largely from her pigtailed hair. Her simple dress left large areas of shapely limb exposed and failed to mask her fully developed figure, thrusting and swelling beneath the stretched doeskin.

Her body betrayed her true age. Despite an elfin-like face, with its suggestion of the mischief of youth, Little Dove was an experienced woman of the world, probably in her late twenties.

Blanche's morale sunk lower as she, too, observed that the squaw who'd been living with her husband was now sizing up her newest lover. Hatred festered within her.

'If the frigging whore takes it into her head to make a play for you — if she cuts you partly loose — ' she murmured bitterly to Jackson, 'you must eliminate her and get us out of here.'

But Little Dove overheard, and knew enough of their language to understand the remark.

'If I cut Jackson loose, I cut out your pleasure-part first!' she promised with a vicious scooping gesture.

The lurid proposal touched a new spark to Blanche's temper.

'It's easy to threaten enemies who have their hands tied,' she snarled with a wealth of contempt. 'Let me loose and give me a knife — then we'd see who'd get her charms slashed first!'

'Hey! Quit it, will you?' Jackson growled. 'The pair of you.'

The fetid atmosphere in the cabin was hard enough to stomach without having to listen to the women's air-tainting animosity. Blanche made to say more, but Jackson stopped her.

'No!' he said in a hard voice. 'Don't talk! You've done enough insult-spitting for a while. Just let it lie, Blanche. We're in a hell of a spot, and that's the truth. Cat fights don't help us a bit.'

But another whole day of this waiting stretched before them at least. He wondered if he could keep them from slitting one another's throats until Angry-fist returned and Kilkieran carried out his promise to hand them over as the maimed and dangerously warped rebel chieftain's prize.

For that matter, was it worth the effort?

13

SEARCH FOR BODIES

Misfit Lil led Covington's troop to Buckmeyer's Ford. The journey took them the best part of the day — a time Lil's grey pony must have halved in her round-about flight from the Apaches to Fort Dennis the previous day.

Coming to the river late in the afternoon, her spirits sank when she saw the wreck of the wagon, on its side in midstream, the canvas drifting like a dirty white shroud in the pull of the current.

Covington surveyed the scene and gave prompt orders. 'Sergeant O'Leary! Split the men into two parties and search both banks downstream.'

'What for?' Lil asked bluntly.

Covington frowned irritably, regarding her presence itself as a kind of interference he preferred to do without.

'To find their bodies, of course,' he snapped. 'It's as plain as the nose on your face what happened. They panicked when they saw Apaches, spilled their wagon and drowned.'

'That's not how I read it, Soldier,' Lil said.

Covington winced. 'It's Lieutenant, as you're well aware, Miss Goodnight. And you'll kindly let me be the judge of what has to be done.'

Lil gave a sigh of frustration. She knew she couldn't change his mind till his men were following his orders and out of earshot.

'Jackson's chances would be a lot better if you weren't so obstinate, Mike Covington,' she grumbled under her breath.

Her concern for Jackson grew in leaps and bounds. She knew it was silly of her to feel the way she did about him. He was many years her senior and she thought she'd managed to repress her emotions, dismissing them as calf-love. And Jackson had made it clear enough on occasion that he didn't consider a relationship between them appropriate, though she knew he admired her myriad skills as an outdoors woman and paid her compliment on them.

Whatever Lil did, however, she couldn't get around it — especially at times like these. Jackson appealed to her female instincts. Because she hadn't been an innocent since she'd rebelled and kicked over the traces when sent to Boston by her father for education of a different sort, the appeal easily escalated into physical reaction, though this was manifested at present only by the knots in her stomach.

Though Lil wasn't a natural dreamer, Jackson filled her mind's eye. The far-seeing pale blue-grey eyes — like a seaman's perhaps — the weather-burnished face, the long, shoulder-length hair, the tidy chin-beard. Tall herself, she appreciated it that he was taller, and wide-shouldered. And as well as physically capable, he was an educated man, knowledgeable of the classics of literature and said to speak seven languages and several Indian dialects.

Jackson was all the things in a man that Mike Covington was not. Ironically, Lil reflected, he (Jackson) saw Covington as a fit candidate for her affections!

Once the troop was at work, searching the river and mussing up such evidence as the ground might yield, Lil tried again to sway Covington.

'If it's like you say, how do you explain the absence of the wagon horses? Are they drowned, too? If so, where are their big bodies?'

'They were spooked — broke free, run off,' Covington blustered.

'Where are they now then?'

'How should I know? Possibly halfway back to their stables in Silver Vein!'

'I don't think so. Look again, Mike, closer. The traces 'pear *cut* to me.'

'Ah! That's it, of course. Farraday

and Mrs Kilkieran freed the team, climbed on them and rode ashore to continue their journey — wherever that was taking them.'

Lil shook her head disconsolately. 'That won't wash either. I seem to remember the livery's two ol' wagon hosses, though docile, were broken only to harness. What's more, I don't reckon the Blanche woman knew how to ride — leastways, not horses.'

Covington coloured, betraying to Lil he wasn't quite as devoid of worldly knowledge as she supposed, but she was in no mood to be really amused. His blushes were more suited to a fourteen-year-old boy than a man grown. How anyone like Jackson could suppose she might like to become romantically involved with Mike Covington, she couldn't fathom. Now Jackson himself, that would be different . . .

She jerked herself out of the reverie. There was important work she had to fix her mind on.

She went on, 'I'm going to see if I

can find some tracks to read before your men have trampled 'em all out of existence.'

She rode slowly away from the ford but kept within a short distance of the river. It was rocky, hard ground clear of the banks, and a freshening east wind shifted dust in a way that obliterated the undisturbed tracks here, but Lil eventually found what she was seeking.

Her keen eyes picked out kicked and rolled rocks; snapped stalks of grass growing in the rare patches of clay. She found a scraped area and moving away from it, parallel sets of heavily indented, probably moccasined footsteps. A party of Indians toting some weighty burden?

A body, dead or alive?

She called Covington over to show him.

'I figure the Apaches took 'em, hosses and all. I'd say by the lady's bootprints I see here and there that a white woman on foot was with them — a woman with a heavy tread.'

'Mrs Kilkieran saw Colonel Lexborough when she visited the fort, so I wasn't personally acquainted,' Covington said. 'Would you describe her as — uh — heavy?'

'Shall we say she was well endowed with fleshy substance? Not muscular, but her upper body and backside were quite large.' Lil's eyes widened at Covington's renewed embarrassment. 'I did have an occasion — limited, of course — to view both unadorned by corsetry or hoop skirts. I'd say a woman of her weight would fit these impressions.'

Covington took off his hat, fanned his cheeks with it and examined its crown with unwarranted attention.

'Lord . . . where are they now?'

'They're probably at Angry-fist's camp long since — the hosses in the cooking pots and Jackson and Blanche Kilkieran dying at the torture stakes!' Lil finished with a vehement cry, shocked by the image she'd raised in her own mind.

Covington swallowed. He never felt comfortable with displays of feeling. 'You don't have to get hysterical, Miss Goodnight.'

'I'm not, but don't you think we've wasted enough time here? You should be riding in on Angry-fist's place — sabres drawn!'

'Out of the question!' Covington snapped, flicking his gauntleted hand dismissively.

Lil flinched and he added in what he meant to be a more conciliatory tone, 'I personally agree the Indians should be in the reservations and the rebels wiped off the map, but I can't initiate aggressive action on a mere girl's say-so. It would be against orders and current departmental policy. Furthermore, it would inflame a previously tense situation.'

'Well, maybe we could do it without the sabres?' Lil ventured.

'I think not. As you've probably noticed, the light's already failing. It would be ridiculously risky and ill-advised. We'll pitch camp here for the night and reconsider options in the morning. Perhaps I'll put together a small party to visit the hostiles under a truce flag in broad daylight.'

Misfit Lil groaned in despair. 'God be merciful!' she breathed to herself. 'Come morning, Jackson could be dead and scalped.'

★ ★ ★

Morning found Jackson Farraday mildly surprised he and Blanche Kilkieran in particular had survived a second night in the Apache camp, this time as the prisoners of Kilkieran's squaw, Little Dove. Surprised because, no doubt about it, the handsome young Indian harboured homicidal intentions toward the white woman.

But she knew she'd have to square the murder with Patrick Kilkieran, whom she served dutifully and respected — feared? — one hundred per cent. So her hand was stayed.

Blanche seemingly couldn't stop herself from goading Little Dove.

'You'll starve us to death, bitch,' she said. She was contemplating lapping gruel, served for their primitive sustenance, from a wooden bowl on the dirt floor.

'We're not pet animals, you know,' she went on. 'You might be the Preacher's kitten, of course, but I was never that . . . Of course, I can imagine what he does to you when you go down on your hands and knees, you sex-hungry, dirty little beast, showing him your naked, stinking little — '

'Blanche, stow it!' Jackson warned.

The taunt, and others that had preceded it, was in the most basic English an unlettered heathen could understand. Blanche had played on the lone girl's fears and pride intolerably, insulting her and daring her to cut her loose and fight out whatever it was between them. Could it really be the worthless affections of Patrick Kilkieran, Jackson wondered?

But this time was different. Little Dove's frayed temper finally snapped. Blanche had gone too far. Little Dove's eyes glittered dangerously and her hands clenched and unclenched. They were the hands of a crazy woman — a beside-herself killer.

Jackson felt anger like hot sour bile at the back of his throat. 'You fool, Blanche,' he said through clenched teeth. 'You won't get us out of here this way.'

Slowly, almost invisibly, a taut smile curved the bronze-faced girl's mouth.

'Very well, white bitch! You shall have your wish. I will cut you loose and give you knife. Then I kill you, and say you try to escape!'

Jackson's heart pounded. He ran a tongue over his dry lips. 'Damnit, Blanche, back down. You can't go through with this. Tell her you didn't mean it. She'll kill us both for sure. There'll be no witnesses.'

Blanche laughed and Jackson realized she'd become more than a mite deranged, too.

'I might have to sit here, Jackson Farraday, but I don't have to listen to you. They weren't going to let us out of here alive anyhow!'

'You'll listen to me for just as long as you have to sit there,' Jackson told her roughly. 'While there's life, there's hope.'

But it didn't sound positive to his own ears, and Blanche made a disbelieving noise.

'I want out now. I don't give a shit what you say. Who do you think you are to offer advice after what you've gotten me into?'

'Someone has to talk sense to you, Blanche. We're not beaten yet!'

She shrugged her rounded shoulders in total weariness. 'Oh, what's the use? Be honest, Farraday. It's as bad as it can get. Don't you understand? I want her to give me the damn knife and get it over with. Just think what they plan to do with me, will you? I'll not wait to be pack-raped by her disgusting red brothers!'

'We'll think of something,' Jackson said. 'We'll get out of here somehow.'

Little Dove turned on him, spitting fire.

'Shut up, long-haired one! She has chosen and I want to kill her! You interfere and maybe I use my knife afterward to amuse me a little . . . to see if all white men made way of Preacher and Apache men!'

She spun around and there was a glitter of light on steel as she whipped a long, bone-handled knife from a leather sheath on a cord at her waist. With two deft slashes, she freed Blanche's ankles and wrists.

Blanche instantly lurched unsteadily to her feet, but Little Dove contemptuously pushed her over and she collapsed weakly into a corner of the cabin.

'You run nowhere yet,' Little Dove said. 'I give you knife of own, then we see if white woman's fight as strong as her words.'

Desperately, Blanche massaged her wrists and ankles. Any second, Jackson expected to see the blade flourished by Little Dove plunged into her.

But the Indian girl made good on her promise. She snatched up a second knife similar to her own from an untidy heap of gear in the kitchen area of the cabin. She held the weapon left-handed by the tip of its shiny steel and swung the hilt at Blanche's face.

'Take it!'

The white woman instinctively raised her hand to protect herself and the horn hilt slapped into her palm. The knife fell to the ground and Blanche tried to back away, although she was already against the rough log wall.

'Take it, or I cut you anyway!' Little Dove hissed. 'I slit skin over big flabby tits so they flop as far as belly!'

Blanche recovered her rash nerve. She looked more like the virago she'd been when needling her husband's squaw. She looked more in command of her swinging emotions — tougher, more capable of killing out of pure malice.

With a screech of suddenly renewed hatred at the Apache girl's insulting threat, she stooped, gathered the offered knife into a white-knuckled grasp, and lunged.

14

BATTLE AT YUMA NAT'S

Yuma Nat Hawkins hadn't felt so uneasy since the day of the bank robbery in Silver Vein. Things had turned seriously sour that day. What should have been a quiet, smooth heist had gone distinctly wrong. There'd been killings and confusion, and the getaway plan had been turned on its head when the gala crowd had stormed back into town with the bluebellies, led by a wild-looking girl with swirling black hair. The gang had been forced to ride out north instead of south.

Still, they'd gotten away all right and the bank's riches were all theirs sure enough. Winter had passed and it was spring. Time maybe to ride out and spend up the money. Whiskey and wild women! The boys would like that. So what was he worrying about now?

Maybe it was guilt. Would he have felt better if he'd been able to send his mother some of the big haul? No, that was stinking thinking. He owed that woman nothing. She'd want nothing of him. Not now, at this late stage in life. The money would cause her problems. She didn't need it anyway.

It was still the small hours and he should be sleeping, not pacing the ranch house veranda nervously. He built a smoke; took some puffs, some more turns, and felt no better.

The moon was sinking toward the horizon in the west and a pale pre-dawn light etched the eastern skyline. It was eerily quiet with not a breath of wind. In the near distance, coyotes called and answered in their mournful howls.

An owl went by. He saw its dark, fleeting shape and heard the flap of its strong wings.

Yuma Nat felt *unsafe*.

Which had to be goddamned foolish-ness if anything was. This was his fortress in the wilderness, his robbers' roost, guarded round the clock in four-hour shifts by seasoned gun hands doing sentry duty from several lookout points.

To intensify his troubles, the old scar that puckered his left cheek — and froze his expression in a grimace or grin that was a constant enigma to associate and enemy alike — began to itch.

* ★ ★

From high on the pink cliffs that backed the ranch house, from behind stands of cedar and scrubbier juniper, from the depths of flanking canyons, the ghostly shapes slithered, materializing out of a desolation where good sense said they could not have been.

Silently, knives rose and fell in brown hands. The outlaw sentinels emitted the briefest of strangled cries. Of pain, shock. Then their bodies went limp and they died with rattling gurgles, mostly drowned in the blood from their own slit throats and punctured lungs.

In a cold half-light, the eerie silence over the land was broken. Raiding parties of whooping, mounted Apaches raced over the dewy flat from three directions and attacked the sprawling ranch house.

★ ★ ★

Lieutenant Covington struck camp almost before the streaks of first light were beginning to broaden in the eastern sky. Misfit Lil thought this was because he appreciated she'd be nagging him if he didn't, and one day of that already had been too much.

It was a small victory.

She'd told Covington he was a damned fool about certain things on occasions before now; could be this time the message had registered. But the success was overshadowed by her fears over the fate of Jackson Farraday since a second night had passed.

Going over it broodingly, Lil toed the

stirrup of her borrowed army horse and swung into the saddle. It was an old service Grimsley that had a significant amount of leather in it and brass fixtures. She considered it uncomfortable — certainly it would be for range work — and wondered whether Covington had arranged its supply out of pique over Colonel Lexborough's decision that she be allowed to guide the troop to the site of the Apache attack on Mrs Kilkieran's wagon.

They'd ridden only a short way toward the last known camp-ground of Angry-fist when Lil and Covington's thirty-strong troop heard a crackle of distant gunfire. They were negotiating the steep side of a hogback ridge that took them from a gully bottom which had promised easier travel but, as Lil had futilely heeded, would lead them into a maze of tricky canyons.

Lil, Covington and some others pushed their horses quickly to the crest to see what the shooting was about.

'Look!' Lil cried. 'An Apache raiding

party on the rampage!'

Covington took in the view. The Indians were circling a ranch house and its outbuildings. The people forted up inside were answering with a barrage of defensive fire, but it was obvious that in such a situation they could hold out only until their supplies of ammunition were exhausted.

Forgetting in the excitement of the discovery that he was shunning Lil's assistance, Covington asked, 'What is that place?'

'The old Stopler ranch that the Hawkins gang has made its nest,' Lil said.

Covington's eyes gleamed with pleasure. Indians attacking white folks. Here was all the justification he needed to defy the order from on high to go easy on the Apaches.

'We'll join the battle and rout the savages!' he declared.

Lil saw it otherwise. 'But they're just trash down there. A bad, murderous lot of thieves and gunmen. They ain't any more civilized than the Injuns! Could be they're getting their comeuppance.'

Her protests were ignored. Covington promptly formed up his men in a strong voice and ordered the bugler to blow the call for the charge.

'Mike!' Lil yelled. 'Those Injuns are Angry-fist's bunch, the same who've gotten Mr Farraday and Mrs Kilkieran. Now's just the time to storm their camp and save 'em.'

'I don't think that course would be fit, young lady. We don't know they're prisoners of Angry-fist — or alive — whereas we have a clear and critical duty here.'

Lil found herself left alone on the ridge. After a swift debate with her conscience, and going against Covington's last instruction to stay put, she rode down in the path of the cavalry toward the furious battle around the Stopler property.

'What for should I save Yuma Nat?' she reflected. 'Well, there *might* be a reason, but it ain't that I'm plumb fond

of outlaws. It's just a crazy hunch I'll
be doing a favour to somebody else I
owe . . . '

* * *

The knives clunked each time they
come together. As weapons, they were
fearsome, the blades curved, fully ten
inches long, and broad. Deadly.

Farraday groaned. He'd long desisted
from his appeals for the women to cease
their struggles. They were intent on
battling to the death. A moment's
distraction for either combatant would
surely bring the fight to a fatal end.

Both women carried numerous super-
ficial wounds, especially to their bare
forearms, where bright globules from
surface cuts mapped the fight's progress
in blood.

Sweat dripped from the pair of them.

Weight and size were on the white
woman's side, but the Apache squaw
was slender and fast, more physically
fit.

'Damn you,' Blanche Kilkieran sobbed. She parried a darting jab from Little Dove with her knife arm and simultaneously lodged a fist in her face. Blood spurted from the native girl's nose.

Little Dove danced back, wiping the back of her hand across mouth and chin, smearing the dripping red hideously.

The pair joined again. The razor-sharp blade edges nicked and grated as they locked. Blanche threw the lighter girl off with a scream of tired rage. She stood ready, waiting for the next darting assault, knife extended like a small sword.

Little Dove dashed forward and thrust, but this time Blanche was not so lumbering in her movements. Moving aside and evading the rush, the tip of her blade also snagged the quick Apache's doeskin dress. The top of the scanty garment ripped, then was torn clean off as Little Dove's momentum carried her past.

The Indian whirled agilely, a line of blood, scarlet on bronze, along her rib cage to the side of her bared right breast. She spat and cursed and sprang again, knife sweeping.

'Now, white cow!'

A howl of pain burst from Blanche as she failed to sidestep the savage slash completely. It took part of her ear and knocked her to the blood-spattered dirt floor.

Little Dove dived on top of her. 'I — slice you — to bits!' she heaved between gasps. 'Rip out soft belly!'

Farraday's heart pounded. The women's bloody knife fight was making him feel physically sick. Nausea churned his stomach. Would this horrific madness never be over?

★　★　★

The Apaches storming Yuma Nat's fortress did not have everything their own way.

Patrick Kilkieran, accompanying them and trying to impose his will on the progress of the operation, saw that whenever the warriors came within a hundred yards of the buildings, a furious blast of firing met them. Several of the mustangs were brought down and a brave with a rusted but well-oiled and prized rifle cursed wrathfully as the stock was smashed into splinters, some of which were driven into his shoulder.

'Hell! There's faster ways to it than this,' the Preacher roared. He didn't intend for his Apache accomplices to have to lay a long siege or fall victim to the outlaw sharp-shooters. *'Burn 'em out like rats!'*

Afterward, he bit his tongue. What if the Apaches did such a good job that Yuma Nat's loot was lost in the fire?

But it was too late to rescind the instruction. A volley of fire arrows rained on the ranch house and its buildings, which were quickly enveloped in smoke and flame.

Then, as the defenders came boiling out, guns firing, a fresh and unexpected development occurred.

A cavalry bugle sounded and a tide of blue-coated riders swept up from beyond the obscuring drifts of fire- and gun-smoke to join battle with the Indians.

Pandemonium took hold.

Kilkieran swore. 'The goddamned army! Now where the hell did they spring from?'

He concentrated his best efforts on losing himself in the milling Apache riders, suddenly caught in a deadly crossfire from the white-men's guns.

Luck seemed to be on his side. Under the cover of the confused, three-cornered conflict, he was able to gain shelter back of the ranch house, where the fire arrows hadn't reached.

Hell, he had to put some ground between him and this godawful mess, but he didn't aim to quit the place without what he'd come for!

Summoning his courage, he darted into the emptied building, his mind fixed on the promise of the Silver Vein bank haul.

Misfit Lil raced downslope, undaunted by the bloodcurdling Apache war cries and the stray, spent lead, yelling like a demon herself.

With both guns drawn, every Indian who rode into her path was a target for Lil. It was payback for the chase of the day before, and it wasn't hard to rekindle her temper when she thought of Jackson Farraday, whom she figured they'd carried off as their captive. Maybe had killed . . .

Her first victim was a redskin whose coloured feathers marked him as some kind of minor leader. The rush took her within a few yards of a knot of the trapped Apaches, guns blazing again. Her coup and bold advance caused the Apaches to hesitate. Seconds later, five of them were on the ground and she was in the midst of the disarray. A survivor tried to close in and strike at her with a tomahawk, but she shot him down. The few left turned tail, howling.

The mêlée brought her up alongside the open door of the old Stopler barn where the outlaws stabled their horses. She was reloading the empty chambers of her six-guns and considering her next move when a man and horse came rocketing out of the inner darkness.

'Hold it, feller!' she called. 'The gunfight ain't over yet.'

But the rider let out a shout of defiance and kept coming. Then she recognized the brutal, scarred face as he sped past, his horse shouldering her own aside.

Damnation, Yuma Nat Hawkins wasn't going to get away!

She spun her borrowed cavalry horse's head and reined into pursuit. They drew away from the battle scene at a hard run, and the chance that either of them might stop a slug or arrow rapidly dimmed.

Although Yuma Nat gave his beast its head, Lil's cavalry mount was better horseflesh and gained ground with almost every pounding stride across the flatland. She bore down on her quarry and pulled alongside. Daringly, she drew her feet from the stirrups and on to the Grimsley saddle. Then she launched herself at Yuma Nat in a flying leap.

Her hurtling weight knocked the gang boss from his horse's back and he had the presence of mind to kick his feet free of the stirrups to avoid being dragged to death by the speeding animal.

The horses ran on loose, till they came to a stop on the dropped reins.

Separately, the riders had tumbled to the hard ground and rolled. They came to their knees twenty feet apart, Yuma Nat spitting dust and snatching up the pistol that had fallen from his holster to lay close by.

He raised it in line with Lil's belt buckle.

'Don't shoot, Hawkins!' Lil begged in a voice sharp and urgent. 'It ain't worth it — I've guessed who you are . . . Ma Coutts's bastard son, stolen away from her by your scoundrel father way back when you were a button. Give her more than your scarless picture to treasure!'

Surprised by her knowledge, Yuma Nat paused as it sank in; the gun muzzle dropped.

'So what?' he finally jerked, breathless. 'Ain't nothin' fer me in that.'

Lil burst out, 'Oh, there is! Confess your crimes and surrender for your sad mother's sake!'

But Yuma Nat was beyond redemption. He laughed coarsely.

'So's she can watch me walk to the gallows? Yuh're crazy! I seen yuh, wild bitch! Ridin' with the soldiers, thar in Silver Vein. Y'all in cahoots — I'm gonna kill yuh!'

His hand raised the pistol again, levelling it.

'Wait! Wait!' Lil cried through stiff lips and feeling curiously numbed.

But Yuma Nat said, 'Go to hell, kid!'

At the last moment, as Yuma Nat's finger whitened round the trigger, Lil flipped the Colt from her right holster too fast for the man's dust-filled eyes to follow.

She shot him. There was no alternative; no time for nicety; no clever, disarming shot.

Her undiscriminating bullet entered Yuma Nat's throat, causing a jet of blood to burst from his open mouth, before drilling through the brain and smashing clear through the skull.

His body seemed to rise in a last reflexive tightening of muscles before it toppled lifelessly on its side like a thrown-down, loose-jointed marionette.

15

PAYING THE PRICE

Misfit Lil put away her six-shooter filled with huge remorse. Back at the Stopler Ranch, Covington's soldiers were trying to save white men. She had killed one. But death came to every man eventually, she tried to console herself.

The reminder served no good other than to bring to consideration another old saw — time waits for no man. Or woman.

While the troopers were rounding up Indian renegades and cleaning out the robbers' nest, the fate of Jackson Farraday and Blanche Kilkieran, the true purpose of their expedition, was going unresolved.

Folly though it seemed, Lil determined to ride on alone to the Apache camp. Weighing in her favour was the clear evidence that most of Angry-fist's fighting force was engaged in the raid on the ranch. It was an opportunity too good to miss.

She went to fetch the powerful cavalry bronc, which was sweaty and dusty but still eager enough to please. She stepped up and threw a leg over the hated Grimsley saddle. The big horse pranced, then broke into a gallop in response to the firm kick in the ribs of her heels.

Lil rode like the wind into the mountains, every nerve in her body tense and ready for the intrusion into Angry-fist's lair. In short time, she was into the lower reaches of the hidden valley, tethering the horse beneath three scraggly cottonwoods by the side of a hole filled with sweet water.

She made her way closer on cautious foot. For the last score of yards, she dropped to the ground and squirmed on her belly Indian-fashion through scrub and brush on the outskirts of the camp.

The place was largely empty, sleepy still, though the sun was a yellow ball way above the skyline. Angry-fist had few women among his band of reservation deserters, but it was these, mostly wrinkled crones who were in the majority here this morning — following the old, free Apache ways, tending cookfires, making corn bread, fetching water and hewing firewood.

Lil was noting with approval the complete absence of little Indian mustangs from the outlying meadow, where they were customarily left to graze, when an unmistakably white voice roared out from the old mountain man's cabin on an overlooking slope:

'*Leave off, you blasted she-devils! What you're doing to one another is purely barbaric!*'

Jackson Farraday! So he was alive. And full of rage and frustration from the great cry she heard. She scooted round the practically deserted camp, not needing to be nearly so wary of discovery.

The Apache women appeared to be indifferent to the noises from the cabin — an indication they'd become accustomed to them over maybe some hours. Lil leaped from the last bit of scanty cover, a cluster of sage, and surged unchecked into the crude dwelling.

A bizarre, jaw-sagging scene greeted her. Jackson Farraday, dishevelled, dirty, beard untrimmed and long hair uncombed, was shoving himself across the dirt floor in jack-knife movements. He was bound hand and foot and progress was erratic. A look of desperation was on his face. His objective was two women who were also on the floor, armed with knives and fighting.

One woman was Blanche Kilkieran, though she was almost unrecognizable. Sweat and spilled blood pasted what was left of her tattered clothing to her fleshy body. Her right cheek had been laid open to the bone.

The other was a hot-eyed Apache girl of about her own age, naked from the waist up, also bloodstained and sweating.

As Lil entered, the Apache got astride Blanche, grasping and pinning her down between her muscular bronze thighs. She caught and forced down Blanche's knife hand to the floor with her left. Her right hand lifted high her own flashing weapon, which was already smeared with blood. Her immediate intention was clearly to bring it down in a violent, lethal plunge.

Farraday's eyes swung. 'Lil, by glory . . . Stop the fools!'

For a moment, it looked like Lil's fortuitous arrival would end the fight at the last critical moment before death was done. She charged toward the two combatants, outstretched hands reaching for the Apache's down-swinging arm.

But she was a fraction too late and merely spoiled the Apache's clean blow to the soft centre between Blanche's ribs. The knife went into Blanche's belly low, impaling itself there as the wielder was lifted off her victim and sent crashing into a corner, Lil on top of her.

The disarmed, bloody Apache threw Lil off and scrambled to her feet. But she was trapped in the corner, at bay, her face contorted with hissing fury.

'What now then?' Lil demanded of her.

Blanche had not risen from the floor behind but was curled up in writhing agony, her hands closed over the hilt of the knife lodged in her vitals. She'd screamed only once before lapsing into sobbing moans.

Baring her teeth in a feral smile, the young Indian came for Lil in a rush, hands crooked like vicious claws. But Lil knew a thing or two about unarmed combat as well as how to use firearms.

She darted aside, grabbed the girl's wrist, and turned her back to her. With a deft heave aided by the girl's own rush, she flipped her over her shoulder.

The cabin's rafters were strung with old, soiled cheesecloth, installed by the original owner as a lining to catch the odd piece of dirt or prairie grass that fell in from the primitive roof. The somersaulting Apache's heels caught in the half-rotted material. It tore till a seam was reached, when the stuff around the girl's whirled legs became a tangle. At the sudden resistance, Lil heard a sickening crack and knew that at the very least her opponent's shoulder had dislocated.

The flipped girl crashed to the floor awkwardly, disabled and in great pain.

'Well, serves you right,' Lil said. 'Not all palefaces are as soft as *her*.'

When she looked round she was horrified to see that Blanche was doubled up in a foetal position, blood seeping from around where her hands clutched over her belly. She was more pallid than ever, and a glassiness in her eyes suggested she was barely conscious. What little agonized sounds she was making were scarcely audible.

God, she's a goner, Lil told herself.

'Quick!' Jackson rapped. 'Cut me loose.'

She rushed to meet his instruction, almost unthinkingly picking up the blood-greasy knife that had been dropped by Blanche.

'What in God's name has happened here?' she asked.

The last time she'd seen Jackson and Blanche they'd been fleeing a blood-thirsty bunch of Angry-fist's renegades aboard the wagon Covington's troop had found wrecked at Buckmeyer's Ford.

Jackson gave her an abbreviated account of their misadventures while she sawed at his bonds.

'You were right about Preacher Kilkieran,' he concluded. 'The rogue saved us from being guests of honour at a scalp dance, but it was only a stay of execution to serve his own dastardly ends in persuading Angry-fist to raid Yuma Nat Hawkins's robbers' hideout.'

'The louse!' Lil said. 'Of all the goddamn gall! He sure knows how to stink up every place he goes — a rebel Indian camp. I should've killed him before he had the chance to quit Silver

Vein, and hang the consequences! Instead, I let him get away before I'd so much as evened the score for what he did to Estelle.'

'We have to see what we can do for his unfortunate wife,' Jackson reminded.

'Sure. She weren't no pretty innocent, but she doesn't deserve what Kilkieran has brought down on her.'

Their concern, and the woman's dire plight, claimed all their attention. They went down to their knees beside Blanche and tried to turn her to look at her wound.

Jackson felt for a pulse.

'Is — is she dead?' Lil asked, horror-stricken anew.

So consuming was their disquiet over Blanche's wretched condition that the sense of another's presence — which is a hallmark of the true frequenter of dangerous places and which each possessed in full measure — warned them an instant too late.

'How unfortunate . . . or should I say fortunate?'

The harsh taunt of derision wrenched their gazes away from the gross but pathetic heap that was Blanche Kilkieran. Framed in the doorway was the surprising sight of Patrick Kilkieran, covering them very completely with a Colt revolver.

'What do you want here?' Jackson demanded. 'You've caused grief aplenty without having to return to gloat over the latest result of your foulness, Preacher!'

'Didn't you get your bloodstained money, mister?' Lil said, having been put in the broader picture by Jackson and bravely employing her own brand of mockery.

'Sure, I got the Silver Vein loot — two bulging saddle-bags of it in unmarked paper money and gold double-eagles.'

'Then why don't you hightail it, you smug sonofabitch?'

'Because I got a last job to do here. Seemed kinda unlikely Angry-fist and his boys would be making it back too promptly and Mr Farraday and my faithless wife might cheat the torture stake, so I have to attend to it myself.

Well, it don't look like Blanche will be needing attention, but your interference brings the number up square again, Misfit Lil.'

Jackson broke in angrily. 'What in damnation are you spouting about, Kilkieran?'

'Just this — I reckon you're the only two whites who could testify against me, so I'm gonna blast you to Kingdom Come before I ride out of the country.'

From the corner where she stoically nursed her injured shoulder, Little Dove, forgotten by everyone, was striving to follow the drift of the palefaces' talk. Alarmed by a flash of insight, she suddenly pleaded, 'Stay and mend broken arm, One-Who-Cures!'

Kilkieran laughed cruelly. 'Don't reckon so, Little Dove. I'm leaving now. I'm a long-gone daddy and I don't need you anyhow. I'm heading across the big water to the fleshpots of Europe. That's no place for an unwashed, cut-up savage.'

Little Dove was devastated. She lurched to her feet and went toward him, oblivious of the gun he fisted.

'I not want to be discarded woman with Apache. Heap bad medicine! Take me with you, One-Who-Cures! Mend broken arm! Heal cuts! Me your squaw — slave forever!'

With this distraction, no one was taking any notice of Blanche. Except Lil. She was wondering if Blanche was already dead, or close to it, when the stricken woman took her bloodied hands from her belly and with a surprising and supreme effort pushed up on to her knees.

Praise the Lord! She lived.

The knife she'd fought with and that Lil had used to cut Jackson loose was now close to Lil's foot, just where it had been dropped when she and Jackson had rushed to tend to Blanche.

Swiftly, stealthily, Lil kicked the knife across the floor to the swaying woman. With bated breath, she followed the glimmer of full understanding that returned to the fatally wounded, hate-filled woman's eyes. Blanche's shaky hand seized up the knife.

She looked at it, and a hideous joy came to her ravaged features.

Kilkieran was shoving Little Dove back. 'Get offa me, dirty Injun whore!' he snarled. 'You're — '

His words broke off in a gurgle of terror.

Incredibly, Blanche had rushed him, thrusting a knife deep into his neck. Crimson fountained spectacularly from the severed carotid artery.

Taking her worthless husband with her into the great unknown of the hereafter was the last and maybe best deed of Blanche's selfish life. For she collapsed on top of him in bloody embrace, dead.

'Hmm!' Lil said. 'Goodbye, fleshpots of Europe . . . hullo, hell. Guess I've gotten even, Preacher Kilkieran.'

From outside came the blast of a cavalry bugle. Lieutenant Michael Covington had arrived.

'You'd think Mike Covington would make it to be in at the finish some time,' Lil said.

'You would think so,' Jackson said.

They were riding back to Silver Vein several hours later.

After a very short silence broken only by the clop of hoofs and the chirp of crickets in the roadside grass, Jackson added, 'But I understand he did clean up Yuma Nat's outlaws and most of Angry-fist's fighters.'

'Huh!' Lil returned dismissively. 'Did you see his face when he saw Kilkieran's half-naked squaw, let alone the corpse of his bloodied wife. What a powder-puff!'

Jackson frowned. 'You're being uncharitable to the lieutenant again. I think he honestly believes a true lady should be incapable of the remotest approach to indelicacy of thought, speech or action. You could do no better than to learn to appreciate his beliefs, Miss Lilian. He's a young man. He's well-educated and qualified — '

'Yeah. And so am I,' said Lil as they jogged along companionably, stirrup to stirrup. 'Spent some time in a Boston seminary for young ladies, remember? It matured me greatly and allowed me to throw off some shackles, though that weren't any of Pa's intention. Now, Mike Covington's time at West Point Academy surely did the reverse.'

Jackson shook his head ruefully. 'I can see I'll never be a matchmaker.'

Lil laughed. 'Get that marrying out of your head! Church bells in the same breath as Mike scare me. Freedom's mighty precious in this land of liberty.'

Then she gigged her horse slightly ahead, lest the hungry, yearning look she was sure was in her eyes should pain him.